The Bookcase Collection

Virginia Henderson

Happy Reading!

This book is dedicated to all my fellow story tellers and word weavers, both published and not published. May words never fail you, and may your pen never run dry.

The names, locations, events and situations in this book are all fictional

Printed 2020

Forward:

Lightening crackled, illuminating the old dark room, allowing Penny to clearly see the portrait of great uncle Morris that hung above the stone fireplace without the help of her flashlight. Great uncle Morris looked a lot like one who might dabble in the art of taxidermy or spend his free time taking leisurely strolls through ominous cemeteries.

Great uncle Morris had a unique style all of his own. His thin, gangling form was enclosed in a stuffy black Victorian-style suit. His striking white hair was combed back and his beard was pointed at the end. The portrait displayed him sitting in a red, high back chair with one leg crossed over the other and his large boney hands folded in his lap. An enormous bookcase took up the space in the background.

Penny shuddered beneath the stern gaze of her great uncle and had to look away. Although it was only a painting and great uncle Morris had passed away many, many years ago, it still gave her chills.

The wind moaned and groaned outside. Limbs from the ancient oak tree blew in the wind, tapping and scratching against the rickety old window. Penny pulled her coat tighter around her and looked around anxiously.

Why would Aunt Winnie want to live in this old place?

Aunt Winnie, the sole beneficiary to great uncle Morris' estate and all its possessions, was gravely ill. Aunt Winnie's doctor firmly believe that the woman was on death's doorstep and no amount of anything could help her. Family and distant relatives had come and gone all day, saying their final farewells and taking self-guided tours of the estate, secretly pinning for two or three priceless antiques to be left for them in the will.

Penny's family had been there since three that afternoon and had only left once for dinner. Penny's mom insisted on staying through the night to make sure that Aunt Winnie wasn't alone during her final hours.

After finishing her homework and getting bored of playing games on her tablet, Penny decided to do some exploring without telling

4

anyone. It wasn't hard to get lost in the maze of rooms and corridors and just about the time she realized this, the storm hit.

In the attempt to find the guest room again, she stumbled across this room. In truth, all the rooms that she'd peeked into looked the same. All of them were dusty, smelled of mildew and the furniture was covered in heavy white drapes. From of the look of things, none of the rooms had been touched in years.

However, this room was very different. For starters, a fire was burning brightly in the fire place. At first this frightened her, but now she found the warmth from the fire comforting. Secondly, this room lacked the white drapes that covered everything, and there was not a cobweb in sight. Aunt Winnie lived alone and was too weak and sickly to move around. Which begged the questions, who started the fire and who spent time in this room?

Penny shined her flashlight on the other side of the room and saw what looked to be the exact same scene from the portrait; the high back chair and the bookcase. The only difference was that this bookcase was empty except for a single book lying flat on the center shelf.

Penny moved closer and studied the book. It wasn't too thick or thin, but just the right size in her opinion. The red cloth covering was old and worn, its corners ripped. Neither a title nor an author's name were visible.

Curiosity getting the better of her, Penny picked up the book and curled up in the chair that turned out to be more comfortable than it looked. Penny carefully opened the book to the first story and began reading.

Table of Contents:

The Reluctant Mermaid...........pg. 10

Homeward Bound Mishap........pg. 18

       Chapter 1.........pg. 19

       Chapter 2.........pg. 23

       Chapter 3.........pg. 28

       Chapter 4.........pg. 38

       Chapter 5.........pg. 43

The Deal...............................pg. 51

       Chapter 1.........pg. 52

       Chapter 2.........pg. 60

       Chapter 3.........pg. 64

       Chapter 4.........pg. 66

       Chapter 5.........pg. 71

The Eternal Shining Star.........pg. 75

       Chapter 1.........pg. 76

Chapter 2………pg.85

Chapter 3………pg. 89

The Diamond Eye Boutique…...pg. 95

Chapter 1………pg. 96

Chapter 2………pg. 99

Chapter 3………pg. 103

Chapter 4………pg. 108

Starlight…………………….pg. 111

Friendship is Stronger………..pg. 114

Chapter 1………pg. 115

Chapter 2………pg. 119

Chapter 3………pg. 124

I'll be Home…………………pg. 127

Chapter 1………pg. 128

Chapter 2………pg. 132

Chapter 3………pg. 138

The Gallows…………………pg. 141

Bullied............................pg. 147

    Chapter 1.........pg. 148

    Chapter 2.........pg. 154

    Chapter 3.........pg. 159

    Chapter 4.........pg. 163

    Chapter 5.........pg. 171

The Rebel..........................pg. 173

    Chapter 1.........pg. 174

    Chapter 2.........pg. 184

    Chapter 3.........pg. 191

    Chapter 4.........pg. 196

Love Letters in the Attic.........pg. 199

    Chapter 1.........pg. 200

    Chapter 2.........pg. 205

    Chapter 3.........pg. 207

Keep Swinging...................pg. 215

The End..........................pg. 219

The Reluctant Mermaid

The foamy waves gently roll over the white sand, only to recede back into the ocean. A glorious pink sunset illuminates the peaceful beach.

The crowds are long gone and not so much as a footprint is left in the sand. Other than a single seagull flying overhead, the only visible sign of life is a petite figure sitting on the water's edge.

The young girl sits cross-legged on the sand. Her flip-flops lay discarded a few feet away where she kicked them off. She digs her toes in the moist sand and revels in the feeling of it. A warm summer breeze blows through her long blonde hair. Her deep blue eyes gaze far out into the water as she fingers her shell necklace. The necklace is both a gift and a curse, the only thing that brought her back to the ocean.

As another wave rolls in, it carries a pleading voice calling out to her. "Please come home, Serena."

Serena feels the urge of the waves as they wrap around her, drawing her in. She resists its tug and the waters slink back.

Serena closes her eyes; salty tears begin to form. She wipes at them, leaving specks of sand on her cheek.

Let me have another day. Just one more day, she begs desperately. *I know the deal was only for the summer, but…I'm happy here.* She doesn't have to speak out loud because the waves will carry her message.

In response, a wild wave comes plowing up to the shore, hitting her with an unnatural force. Its power whips her around and nearly carries her out to sea.

Neither her nose nor the back of her throat burns from swallowing the salty water. A burning sensation would be better than what she's feeling.

Serena's insides tighten up and she feels her heart breaking, knowing that she can't withstand the inevitable forever. She sighs deeply, thinking back over the last couple of months.

Under the guise as a summer exchange student from overseas, Serena was given a temporary home with the Davens. The Davens are a close-knit, fun family who welcomed Serena with open arms and hearts.

Serena made friends with Melissa, the youngest of the three Daven children. She and Melissa hit it off when Serena complimented Melissa's stick figure drawing of a mermaid sitting on a rock combing her hair.

"It's a beautiful picture. But mermaids don't only sit around brushing their hair. They do all kinds of things."

Melissa's large eyes bore into Serena's intensely. "What else do mermaids do?"

"Everyday things, just like you. They go shopping, eat at restaurants, play at the park. And on special occasions, there's the Orca Opera. Mermaids swim from miles and miles just to hear the enchanting music. Mermaids love music, you know."

From that day on, Melissa became Serena's shadow. The five-year-old would smile up at her with reverence and hold her hand when they went on outings. Many times, Melissa would beg Serena to tell her more about mermaids and the child gobbled down every word, her imagination running wild.

When Serena wasn't spending time with the Daven family, she did her best to blend in with young people her own age. After all that was why she was there; to experience what it was like be a human.

One day in late June, Serena was sitting by herself in the food court at the mall drinking a slushie and causally observing the teenagers around her. Groups of four or five clustered together, chatting, texting, and showing each other something on their phones.

Suddenly, something caught her eye. At a small table nearest a trash can, a girl was sitting alone; nervously eating a soft pretzel as if she were terrified someone would snatch it away if they saw her eating.

There was something different about this girl. She didn't hold herself confidently and proudly like the others. She kept her eyes down and her shoulders hunched.

Serena decided right away that this was the girl she wanted to befriend. Taking her slushie and handbag, she stood up and calmly approached the girl.

"Hi, I'm new here. My name's Serena."

The girl gaped; astounded that someone was actually addressing her. And not nastily either.

14

"Hi. I'm Pamela, but I go by Pam."

Serena smiled. "Do you mind if I sit with you?"

Pam's eye lit up and for the first time in a long time, she genuinely smiled. "Sure, if you really want to."

From that day on, Serena and Pam became friends. They spent the summer at the mall, the arcade, the carnival, and the movies.

One of Serena's fondest memories was when she invited Pam to a cookout at the Davens. They played badminton, corn hole, enjoyed an amazing lunch, and in the evening, they roasted marshmallows over the fire pit in the back yard.

The wind suddenly picks up and Serena notices how cold the water is now. She pushes aside her thoughts, knowing she can't keep stalling. She has to return before dusk. Those were the terms. Unfortunately, when she agreed to those terms, she had no idea how much it would hurt to carry them out.

Saying her goodbyes that morning was one of the hardest things she's ever done.

Serena digs her fingers and toes through the sand before giving in and accepting reality.

Reluctantly, Serena stands up and walks into the water. The waves gush and splash around her like an excited puppy.

Deeper and deeper she goes. When the water is waist high, she turns and takes one final glimpse of the beach before diving into the sea.

The familiar tingly sensation runs up and down her body as it had that first summer day, such a short time ago. Swapping her legs for a tail feels unnatural at first, but then it's like meeting up with a long-lost friend and she wonders why she didn't miss it before. Her tail is pink, similar to the pink cotton candy from the carnival, and her scales shimmer when light from the surface touches them.

Not far off her sisters beckon her. They would swim to her, but a mermaid can only get so close to shore before they begin to forget who and what they are. More than once, a curious mermaid drifted too close and never returned home. Serena, however, was given her memory in the form of a shell necklace and admonished to never take it off, lest she never return home.

It doesn't take long for her to get the knack back for swimming and before long she's gliding gracefully through the water towards home.

The further she goes, the less pain she feels from leaving her friends until it's nothing more than a hazy memory and she wonders if she dreamt it all.

End

Homeward Bound Mishap

Chapter 1

Gazing out the plane window, I look out into the deep Atlantic Ocean. Uncharted and undiscovered- to dive down and unlock mysteries would be thrilling. But I'll leave that task to another. I've had enough adventures to last a while.

I pull out a weather beaten and badly tattered picture from my cargo pants pocket. The top right corner is missing but this picture has gotten me through many hopeless nights. The picture was taken at last year's family reunion.

My beautiful wife, Ellen. Words can't express how much I've missed her. There were so many times during this mission that I thought for sure I'd never see her again.

My oldest boy, Jackson, is eleven and wants to grow up so fast he can't stand it. Before I left, I showed him how to clean, load, and shoot a gun. It might sound crazy, letting an eleven-year-old learn to use a gun, but Jackson is mature for his age and he understands that a gun is not a toy.

Michael, however, is nine and is content to lay on the floor and color pictures of superheroes as he watches cartoons and munches cereal. The boys are polar opposites.

I tuck the photo back in my pocket and settle comfortably in my seat to enjoy the ride and catch up on some sleep. The pilot said it would take a couple hours before we reach the ship that will take me the rest of the way home to Florida.

Before I left Venezuela, my supervisor, Mr. Riley, told me that the worst was behind me and to take it easy for a couple weeks and don't worry about a thing. I deserve the rest. Despite his words I could tell from his tone and body language that he wasn't very happy with the outcome of my mission; I can't say that I blame him.

I was sent to retrieve a priceless diamond deep in the Amazon rainforest that's said to have uncanny abilities. I never so much as saw a speck of it. Either someone must have gotten to it first or it was only a myth.

I suppose I should count my blessings. I barely escaped with my life after being discovered by a hunting party of cannibals. I was kept a prisoner in a hut, awaiting my execution.

It was only after obtaining a shard of broken pottery that I was able to cut my bonds and steal away after dark. When I close my eyes, I can easily visualize that horrifying night. How fast my heart raced in my chest; I was so sure that I would be discovered. I tripped and stumbled over vines and tree roots, weak from lack of sleep and nourishment.

Then my worst fear came to pass. The cannibals found out that I escaped and the hunt was on. I recall the torches, hundreds of torches, burning bright as day, dancing through the jungle searching for me. I was able to find shelter in a hollow tree trunk, which was uninhabited, and the natives eventually gave up the search and returned to their village.

During that week I survived mostly on berries that I knew to be edible. I fashioned myself a spear and after several depressing tries, I managed to get a quail. I built a pitiful fire and the meat lasted until I made it safely out of the jungle. The days were steamy and hot but nights were slightly cooler and, despite my predicament, I did manage to sleep some at night but not deeply. It would have been foolish to let my guard down for even a second.

But like Mr. Riley said, the worst is behind me and I can look forward to the next two weeks with my family.

This thought is enough to push aside any and all cares and anxieties. My eyes grow heavy and the last thing I remember seeing is a glimpse of the endless ocean below.

Chapter 2

I don't know how long I slept, but I wake up feeling groggy, like I just drank a bottle of cough syrup. My throat is dry and my head is pounding.

Suddenly there's a high pitch squeal and through blurry vision, I see a light flashing on the dashboard. The flight is no longer steady and we're swerving as if the pilot has lost control.

From my seat in the back, I lean forward and shout, "What's wrong?"

"Engine trouble! Hang on, I'll straighten her out," he calls back.

Still stupid with sleep, I make sure my seat belt is on good and tight. I don't know much about flying, I'm not even sure what kind of aircraft this is, so there's nothing I can do but trust that the pilot knows his job.

The pilot announces, "Something's wrong with her! We might have to jump for it, can you swim?"

Sure, I can swim. I've got an in-ground pool at the house. The kids love it. I look down at the dark waters below. But there's a big difference between a pool and the untamed ocean.

"What about the ship that's waiting? Can't you make it there?"

"Under normal circumstances, maybe. But-"

His words are cut off when bullets whiz through, shattering a window and hitting the pilot. Glass sprays and my initial reaction is to duck for cover. Violent wind rages inside the plane. Papers blow around erratically and the seatbelts rattle in the wind. The aircraft is completely out of control now.

After a moment I come to my senses and unbuckle. Staying as far away from the window as a possible, I check the pilot for a pulse.

Nothing. My fingers come back stained with blood. Without a pilot we're going to crash.

Not we, me. I'm going to crash. Unless I jump.

Without a moment to lose I frantically begin searching for a parachute. I don't even realize that whoever shot at is us, is gone. I find a chute under the co-pilot's seat and hurriedly put it on. At least, I assume it's a parachute. It looks like a backpack with some extra straps and buckles.

I struggle to open the door and freeze. Looking down at a watery grave my stomach threatens to lurch.

Before I can really comprehend what I'm about to do, I jump.

The wind rushes in my face as I fall through the air. Some people might think this is exhilarating and I have to question their judgment. I've pulled some crazy stunts before, but this tops them all.

I'm not sure exactly how soon you're supposed to pull the cord. I start to mentally count down from ten seconds but I chicken out and pull the cord before I even make it to six. I feel my body jerk back when the chute flies out but then I'm sailing easily in the wind.

This would almost be enjoyable if it weren't for the fact that I'm hovering over the ocean with no land in sight. I look to the skies. Whoever shot the pilot is long gone.

The plane is dangerously close to crashing. I watch as it hits the water. It submerges before resurfacing upside down and staying afloat.

I instantly put it into my head to swim to it as soon as I land. Until then I try to take stock of my situation as I get closer and closer to landing.

Someone obviously wanted us dead. But why? It's not like I had anything of value on my person. I was just on my way home, not bothering anyone. Maybe someone thinks I did have something. The diamond, perhaps? If I'd found that my supervisor would have it right now, not me. I'm just the delivery boy. The middle man.

My feet hit the water first and I gasp from the sudden cold. I plunge beneath, getting a mouthful of water, and fight to break through the surface. When I do, I'm coughing, sputtering and gasping for breath at the same time. If I wasn't awake before, I am now. I struggle to take off the backpack. The parachute strings are all in tangles.

"Wonder where that ship is," I mutter. My teeth chatter from the cold and it's all I can do to swim back in the direction of the plane. With any luck it will still be afloat and maybe

I can climb onto it. Anything to get out of this freezing water.

I'm not sure how long I've been swimming but my arms and legs are aching and my whole body is numb from the cold. To be honest, I don't even know if I'm going in the right direction anymore. All I know is that if I stop now, I may not be able to start again.

I'm so overcome with exhaustion that I think I'm starting to see things that aren't real. A speed boat is coming towards me, but what would a speed boat be doing out in the middle of the Atlantic?

The engine sounds real enough and I hear someone calling out to me, but a rescue like this would be too good to be true. Someone jumps in the water beside me and before I know it, I'm being hauled up in the boat. I feel a blanket being wrapped around me but I'm already chilled to the bone and the blanket does little but keeps the wind off me.

Chapter 3

I'm half in and out of consciousness, catching bits and pieces of a conversation, but mostly I hear the powerful motor as it cuts across the ocean, spraying water and jolting its passengers.

The next thing I know, it's quiet and I'm lying on a cot. I sit up too quickly and have to lie back down and close my eyes. I'm not deathly cold anymore. My wet clothes have been replaced with a sweater and jeans, both too big for me.

Slowly, I try sitting up again and am rewarded with only a mild case of nausea and lightheadedness. The cot creaks beneath me as I move to stand and am overcome with dizziness. Nope, it's too soon to stand up.

Just then, a man enters the room. Through blurry vision, I note the pristine white uniform, paunch belly and curly black beard. As he comes closer, I see that his nose is badly crooked.

"Glad to see you're finally awake, son. You sure gave us a scare."

I have to clear my throat and even then, my voice is thin and hoarse. "Where am I?"

"My apologizes, I'm Captain Vinny and you're aboard The Steamer. We watched a plane crash and I sent some of my boys to look for survivors. Were there any others with you?"

I slowly shake my head. "Just me and...the pilot." I watch as his death replays in my mind.

"I'm afraid my boys didn't find any pilot. I'm sorry, son." He sighs and continues. "I bet you're near starved. Let's go to the galley for supper."

Supper? It wasn't even noon when we left Venezuela. I don't make a move to stand. "What time is it?"

"Nineteen hundred hours. For land lubbers like yourself, that's seven o'clock."

"I don't know if I could eat, but I would like some coffee if you have any."

"Coffee it is then!" he cheerfully agrees. "You just relax and I'll bring a fresh pot. We can talk more then."

29

Once I'm alone I cautiously get to my feet. I notice a porthole and stumble over to it. Looking out, all I see is ocean, ocean and more ocean. No land in sight. I have no idea where I am and I don't know what to make of the Captain just yet. He seems friendly enough, but I've had my share of two-faced encounters to know better than to blindly trust a stranger.

Captain Vinny returns with a tray containing a pot of fresh coffee, packets of creamer and sugar, stirrers and two foam cups.

He sits the tray down on a side table and brings it in front of the cot. "Glad to see you up on your feet already, son."

I leave the porthole and have a seat on the cot. Captain Vinny pours the coffee and hands me a cup. The warmth from it is blissful.

"Creamer and sugar here if you want. I prefer mine black." He takes a sip. "So, tell me about yourself, son. What brings you out in the middle of the Atlantic?"

If this is his idea of small talk, it's too forward. I busy myself with stirring in creamer so I don't have to meet his gaze. I take a sip and add more creamer.

"Actually, I was wondering if you could tell me where exactly I am. I was supposed to meet a ship to take me to Flor- "

I'm interrupted when Captain Vinny barks out a laugh. He notices my confusion and explains. "Didn't you know, son? You're aboard the ship that was supposed to pick you up. You're Warren Smith, right?"

"Yes..." I can't hide the hesitation in my answer.

"Then that settles it! You've had a bad time of it so far, but it looks like the worst is behind you now."

As much as I would like to believe this, I can't. Something about this Captain and the conversation isn't sitting right. "So, I'm on my way home?"

The Captain nods. "We're on course and should have you home safe and sound tomorrow."

I suddenly have this urge to go on deck and see for myself where we are. "Do you have a phone or radio that I can use to call my supervisor? He said I have to call him once I'm on the ship." This, of course, is a lie, but there's no way he can worm himself out of it. Not only could I double check with Mr. Riley but I might be able to see the course and see for myself where we are.

"You mean Mr. Riley? Called him up the other day when we fished you out of the water. You had a bad case of hypothermia, you know. He told us to let you rest up and to not bother calling."

Well, he slinked around that. And…wait, how did he know my supervisor is Mr. Riley? Unless he really did talk to him. And what did he mean by, the *other day* when they fished me out. What day is it? How long have I been out? I'm thinking too hard now and a headache is forming.

"Why don't you lie down, son. You've hardly touched your coffee. Suppose I'd be feeling the same way too. Get some sleep and I'll wake you for breakfast."

He sets my cup on the table and takes the tray as he leaves. I lay down and stare at the metal ceiling, my eyes fight to stay open. Something is wrong. I can't lay my finger on it, but there's something very distrustful about the Captain. Just before sleep takes me, the door creaks open, a small figure peeps their head in and then leaves as quickly as they appeared.

In the morning, I wake up to the boisterous voice of Captain Vinny announcing that breakfast is ready. My head is a little woozy but I'm able to walk to the door with no problems.

I follow the Captain down the hall. He leads me into the galley where a feast is waiting: scrambled eggs, bacon, sausage patties, and biscuits.

"This is some spread. Expecting more company?" I ask nonchalantly.

"Nhaw, just you and me. My granddad always used to say that you can't conquer the world without a hearty breakfast."

We sit across from each other and I start to fill my plate with a bit of everything. I'm positively starving! I tear open a biscuit in half and start to pile it with eggs and sausage to make a sandwich, when the door opens.

A member of the crew enters and hands Captain Vinny a note. The newcomer doesn't look my way, but I'm too busy devouring my sandwich to really pay attention to what's going on. I look up to see the Captain folding the note in half, a thoughtful expression on his face. The crew member is already gone.

"News?" I ask between mouthfuls.

Instead of answering my question, he says, "Something else my granddad also used to say. Never lie to a dying man if you can help it."

I swallow hard and almost choke on the dry biscuit. I could kick myself for being so careless and letting my guard down. I should have tried to escape last night!

I'm suddenly staring at the end of the barrel of a gun.

I carefully hold up my hands and scan the table for a weapon. A knife would be good. I'd even settle for a fork. That's when I realize that all the utensils are plastic. A lot of good those will do. I'll have to try to reason with him.

"Why would you save my life, only to kill me in cold blood?"

34

"Because Mr. Riley wanted you alive then. And now he doesn't. Stand up and face the wall."

My head is spinning. Mr. Riley wants me…dead? This can't be right. I don't believe it for a second and I tell him so. He abruptly stands up and forces me to stand in the corner, my back to him.

"Let's not make a big to-do out of this. Just accept the facts for what they are. Mr. Riley says you're a liability because you know too much."

I'm trying to listen but I'm trembling with fear. I've gotten out of close scrapes before but I can't see any way out of this one. It would take a miracle. I start to say silent goodbyes to my family when the Captain cocks his gun.

"This isn't personal, son. Orders are orders."

The gun goes off. My heart catches in my throat and I squeeze my eyes, waiting to feel the pain. Nothing happens. I open my eyes and slowly turn around. It's like time has frozen. The Captain is standing there, the gun still in hand, but there's something wrong with him. Suddenly he crumbles to the ground and I see the crew member, the same one who'd just delivered the note, standing behind him with a gun. It takes me a moment to realize what just happened and even when I do. I still can't fully understand.

The man urges me to follow him. "There's no time to lose. Come with me!"

I stumble along blindly; questions buzz around in my head but it seems like I'll have to wait for answers. I stop in my tracks when it dawns on me that he's preparing to leave on a speedboat.

"What are you doing?" I ask.

"Escaping. Unless you want to be here when everyone finds out the Captain's dead," he snaps back.

I don't reply. When he tells me to climb in, I obey. What else can I do? I'm aware that I could be walking into a bigger trap, but the man looks scrawny enough. I could probably take him on if it came down to it. The gun might be a bit of a problem though…

Once we're settled, he turns on the engine and we take off, leaving the ship and all its problems behind.

36

I have to shout to be heard over the motor. "Won't they come after us when they notice we're gone?"

"That's going to be a little hard considering I took all the keys." He holds up a ring of five or six keys and jingles it. "Just leave everything to me and don't touch anything. We've got a lot of ground to cover."

I can't resist adding, "Don't you mean we've got a lot of ocean to cover?"

He gives me a dirty look. "Don't make me regret saving your life."

Chapter 4

"The only thing you need to know about me is that I'm on your side."

This is an unsatisfactory answer to my simple question, what's your name? I don't fully trust him. But to be fair, he doesn't have that same sinister personality as Captain Vinny did.

"I need more than that. If you won't tell me your name, then tell me where I am, how you're involved and why I was almost killed."

He doesn't so much as glance at me. Maybe he didn't even hear me. My throat is getting sore from shouting to be heard over the loud motor.

"Hey, you! Did you at least think about bringing some lunch? I didn't exactly have breakfast."

He relents and we come a slow stop. "Didn't have breakfast? I saw you wolfing down those eggs this morning." He checks his watch. "But I guess it is lunch time. And we've covered enough *ocean* to take a break."

38

He pulls out a backpack behind him and hands me a bottle of water, and a protein bar. "Easy on the rations. They need to last until we reach Florida."

I start to open the protein bar. "How much further do we have to go?"

"If we keep up our current speed, and if there's no delays or problems, we might make it tomorrow afternoon."

"Tomorrow afternoon?" This wasn't what I wanted to hear at all. "I guess the ship was never on course for Florida then."

The man takes a small drink of water. "Correct. They were heading back to Venezuela. Something about your failed mission. I don't know all the details but I do know that he doesn't need you anymore. I read that in the note."

I take a sip of water and find it refreshing, even though it's room temperature.

"Which means..." he continues, "we need to get you to the states pronto. Unfortunately, that would be the first place they would think to go looking for you but it's a risk we'll have to take."

39

"Who would be after me?" I regret my question the second it leaves my lips. He shoots me look that makes me feel small and stupid.

"Haven't you been paying attention? Riley wants you dead, why I don't know, but he does. When he finds out that you're still alive, he's going to send people after you to finish the job." He shakes his head in disgust. "And you call yourself an adventurer."

"I never said I was an adventurer," I argue back.

"You didn't have to. Now are you finished eating? We don't have time to waste sitting idle."

I stare at him, not sure what to think or believe anymore. "Why should I trust you or believe a single word you say? I can't even trust my supervisor now and I've known him for years."

"I saved your life, didn't I?"

I meet the stranger's gaze and hold it. "Captain Vinny saved my life too. You see how that turned out."

My point hits home. We take off again, the speedboat cutting through the waves at a rapid pace. After a few minutes, he shouts over the motor, "You can call me Mike."

The day drags on as we speed across the ocean. By now I'm wet and cold and the constant wind doesn't help. At least I'm not *in* the water though. Mike doesn't say much except to shout out how much closer we are every hour or so. I suppose I should be grateful but honestly, I couldn't be more concerned.

This whole thing could be a huge misunderstanding. What if Captain Vinny was lying the entire time and Mr. Riley doesn't even know where I am? I play around with this theory but have to discard it. The Captain knew Mr. Riley's name. How could he have known? But if Mr. Riley never wanted to me to make it home, why send me off on a plane? Of course, the plane was shot down...

What was it the Captain said? I'm a liability because I know too much? I scratch my head trying to think what that could mean. If all this is referring to the diamond, I couldn't find, they're wasting their time.

My thoughts are interrupted when Mike taps me on the shoulder and points ahead. "About ten hours or so left. You should get some sleep."

I stubbornly shake my head. The last thing I'm doing is falling asleep. Mike may have told me his name, if that even is his real name, but that doesn't mean I'm going to throw all caution to the wind.

My mind travels to my family. Just this morning I believed I would never see them again, and now I'm racing home towards them. I'm tempted to pull out my picture but I don't want the wind to grab it…

Suddenly it dawns on me! I frantically search my pockets. Just as I feared, empty. I'm still wearing the oversized clothes. My clothes are back on the ship. My picture is with them.

I can't begin to describe the temptation that comes over me to make Mike turn around and head back to the ship, but that would be foolish. I'll be home soon. Besides, they probably threw the clothes away by now.

Chapter 5

I can't believe it. I fell asleep. When I get home, I really need to catch up on all my lost sleep. Home...

I sit up straight and look around. We're still in the speedboat, but I can see land in the distance. I tap Mike's shoulder and shout, "Is that it?"

He nods the affirmative and holds up three fingers. As in three hours? I hope it's only three hours. It almost seems too good to be true. After everything that's happened, it seems like there ought to be at least one more disaster. Like the engine dying or running out of fuel...No! Don't think like that. Not when I'm so close.

I glance at Mike. Has he really been awake this whole time? He doesn't even look tired.

The hours pass slowly until we finally make it to Florida. It all feels like a dream.

For some very odd reason, there's a car waiting for us. Mike doesn't give an explanation and I don't press for one. Too many strange things have happened over the last few days. I give Mike directions to my house. It's a relativity short drive. I'm beginning to wonder exactly who Mike is and who he works for. Was it wise to tell him where I live? Maybe. Maybe not. At this point I just want to get home.

Pulling up alongside the curb I anxiously look around. Nothing seems amiss. The sprinklers in the yard are doing their job. Michael's bike is laying in the driveway, nothing unusual about that. I get ready to jump out and dash to the door, but Mike stops me.

"Don't be so hasty. Be alert. If you've got a bad feeling or if something's wrong, stand at the door, thank me for the ride and call me Stan and I'll know there's something up. Otherwise just go in and shut the door."

I tilt me head in confusion. "What could be wrong?"

"Think about it. If someone wants to get at you, who are they going after first? Family, loved ones, the people you care about the most."

I hadn't thought about that. What if my family is in danger? Suddenly I'm thankful to

44

have Mike on my side. Or at least I'm
assuming he's on my side.

"Thanks for getting me home." I feel it's
the least I can say after everything that's
happened.

"You aren't home yet," he answers back.

My excitement deflated, I get out of the
car and carefully walk up the sidewalk. So
far, so good. The door is locked. I only knock
twice before the door flies open and Ellen
embraces me tightly. She's crying. Between
the tears she is saying how much she's missed
me.

Ellen's never cried like this before. She is
trembling in my arms. Over her shoulder I can
see in the living room. Michael and Jackson
are both on the couch, sitting perfectly still
and quiet. I know something's wrong.

I pull away from Ellen and look back at
Mike. He's still parked at the curb, watching
me. "Thanks for the ride, Stan!"

He waves and drives away. I pray he heard
me and understood. I follow Ellen inside and
the door closes behind me.

I turn, ready for a confrontation. Mr. Riley's gun is staring me down. He orders Ellen to sit down on the couch, never taking his eyes off me. I always used to think my supervisor was a nice guy. A bit crazy and a lot eccentric, but overall, harmless. Am I a bad judge of character or what?

"You're a hard man to kill, Warren," he says in an almost friendly manner.

"And you're an even harder man to avoid. What's this all about? I don't have anything that's worth killing for."

Anytime now, *Stan*, I'm thinking anxiously. I thought for sure that he would jump in and give a hand by now. Unless he's gone for help.

Mr. Riley shakes his head. "That's where you're wrong, my friend. You have exactly what I *don't* want you to have."

I don't even try to pretend to understand that statement. "And what would that be?"

"The location of the diamond."

I can't believe this. "I told you before, I don't know where the diamond is. I never found it. Your map was faulty."

His face breaks into a devilish smile.
"You really don't know, do you? I didn't
either at first. Until I did some more digging.
There are several accounts of people who've
went in search of the diamond and some
never returned while others came back with
wild, fictitious accounts. Ask me why this
happens."

"Okay, why?"

Giddy with joy, he answers, "The diamond
protects itself from thieves by swiping and
disordering memories. You found the
diamond alright, but you forgot you did."

I frown in confusion. "But how would *you*
know I found it if I don't even remember?"

Mr. Riley's gun is shaking in his unsteady
grip. "You don't remember anything, do you?
About your little adventure. You came
crashing through the jungle declaring you
were being chased by headhunters. There
were no headhunters. No wild beasts. The
diamond did a real number on you. It's a
wonder you ever made it back."

I shake my head, trying to make sense out
of this. It can't be true. The memories were so
real.

"Even if that's true, why kill me? I have no intention of going back for it or telling anyone else about it."

"No? But you would tell the authorities that I murdered your pilot. And that I ordered that brainless sea captain to kill you. And now I'm threatening your family." He looks in their direction. "I guess that means all of you are a liability."

Mr. Riley's unstable and there's no telling what could set him off. I don't move from my spot. I tell my wife and kids not to move as well. Ellen and the boys are clinging to each other. Jackson is the only one who hasn't shed a single tear. He's afraid but he's angrier than anything. He's also hiding something beneath a pillow on his lap.

The tension is building so much that the air is thick with it. All of us are on edge. Movement on my left catches my attention. Pedro, our cat, is silently approaching Mr. Riley. When he rubs against Mr. Riley's leg, Mr. Riley lets out a scream and jumps back, nearly dropping his gun.

Jackson takes the opportunity to pull out a gun from behind the pillow, *my* gun, and cocks it. "Drop your gun or I'll shoot."

Mr. Riley regains composure and laughs. "You're what? Seven? You don't even know…"

His words are cut short when Jackson fires the gun. The bullet comes within inches of his face and hits the tall lamp next to him, knocking it to the floor.

As if he senses my question, Jackson says, "I've been practicing while you've been gone, dad. Go call the cops. I'll hold him here."

I don't hesitate. It seems like an eternity before the police finally arrive. Jackson lowers his gun only once the police are on the scene. Mr. Riley is handcuffed and swiftly taken away. My family and I are briefly questioned and told to come to the station to give a full report. It turns out Mr. Riley had been there since that morning. What started out as an unexpected visit, turned into an ugly nightmare.

Mike never did show up to help, which leaves me wondering whose side he was really on or if he just liked to jump in and give a hand when it suited him. If it weren't for the cat and Jackson's quick thinking, I don't know what might have happened.

After all is said and done and we're back home from the police station, I pat Jackson on the back and say jokingly, "Looks like you don't need me to teach you anything else when it comes to shooting."

Jackson smiles sheepishly. "Don't be too sure about that. I was aiming for his foot, not the lamp."

End

The Deal

Chapter 1

The new typist is annoying. From the way she only uses her pointer fingers to the way she loudly smacks her chewing gum. It's grating on my nerves.

"Mr. Westcott?"

I whip my head around in the direction of the secretary who called my name. Her name's Linda. She's the only woman I know who still wears victory rolls religiously. I always wondered why a nice girl like her worked for scum like DeVito.

"Mr. DeVito will see you now," she says.

I pick my hat up from the chair beside me and walk towards the office. Linda stops me by the arm.

"Watch what you say. He's in rare form today," she quietly warns.

I smile slyly and straighten my tie. "I always watch what I say."

Linda's expression darkens. "He's got his gun sitting on his desk."

Oh. I shrug as if this news doesn't worry me a bit. I knock on the door before I open it. The room still reeks of cigar smoke and bad liquor, just like it always did.

"Mr. DeVito? You wanted to see me, sir?"

"Get in here and close that door." His accent is still as thick as I remember. A blend of Italian and Brooklyn, loud and threatening.

I do as I'm told and start to take a seat when he says, "Did I tell you that you could sit down?"

Linda wasn't kidding. I notice the handgun sitting on his desk and decide not to do anything to push my luck. "No, sir."

I remain standing while the man puffs on his cigar and stares me down. After a minute he turns and looks out his window. His office is on the sixth floor and overlooks a little Italian neighborhood.

One time, when the boss was in a cheerful mood after getting rid of the eldest son of his most dangerous competitor, he confided in me that it gave him great joy looking down on that neighborhood and watching them go about their lives. For him it's like revisiting family back in Italy.

But now is not the time to bring this up. Now is the time to stay silent until asked to speak.

"It's been a long time, Steve," he states.

"Yes, sir. Three years."

Mr. DeVito faces me. "Three years ain't nothing compared to the twelve years I've spent fighting to stay on top." He pauses and asks, "You read yesterday's paper?"

"Of course, sir." That was a ridiculous question. Who doesn't read the paper?

"Then you saw the article about me. Tell me, what did you think?"

I rack my brain, trying to think back to an article that mentioned anything to do with Mr. DeVito. I would have remembered that. Unless he's talking about…

"You mean the one about the chief of police?"

Mr. DeVito smiles proudly. "One of my top boys did the job and they left a spotless trail. Too bad we didn't get any credit. I could do with a little recognition from time to time."

"What did the chief of police do to deserve...that?"

The headline read, 'Unfortunate End for Beloved Chief.' He'd been attacked in his own house while he was eating breakfast. Authorities said he drowned in his own cereal and that was what killed him.

Mr. DeVito sputters at my question. "What did he do? What *didn't* that nosey pest do? He's always been underfoot, snooping around the place, even back when you worked for me. He was getting closer and closer. Just last week he was up here questioning Judy, asking who her employer is and what's he do. If I hadn't intervened, we'd be done for by now."

"Who's Judy?"

"The typist. I'm thinking about letting her go. She's terrible."

I nod my understanding. "Congratulations then. But you didn't call me in just to tell me that." Honestly, part of me wouldn't be surprised if that was the case. DeVito is shameless when it comes to bragging.

"You're right, Steve. Have a seat and I'll tell you why you're here."

Finally! I gratefully sit down and wait for him to continue. Instead of staying something, he gets up and goes to the large cabinet where he keeps his supply of liquor. He returns to his desk with two glasses and a half empty bottle.

"Let's have a drink while we talk business."

Warning bells go off. Mr. DeVito never offers anyone a drink unless he's going to talk about a job. To him, toasting a drink is the same as shaking on a deal or signing a contract.

"Sir, before you go any further, I want to remind you that I've retired. I don't do jobs anymore."

"That right?" he asks as he pours me a drink and pushes it toward me.

"Yes," I firmly reply.

"Then why did you come when I called?" He barks out a laugh. "Face it, Steve. You came running back like a dog to his master."

I didn't appreciate being compared to a dog. "If that's all, I'll be going then."

Before I can stand to my feet, DeVito has his gun aimed at me. He's not laughing anymore.

Slowly I sit back down. Mr. DeVito nods and puts the gun down but keeps it handy. "That's better. Since you're in such a hurry I'll get to the point."

He slides a file folder across the desk towards me. "I want you to memorize everything about this guy. Where he works, what he does for fun, his family's schedule. I want you to know where he is every minute of every day. I want him gone before Sunday, got it?"

Uh-oh. DeVito never gets this excited about someone unless they're bad news or a serious threat.

"What'd he do to get his own file?"

DeVito downs the rest of his drink before answering, "He dumped a full ashtray over my lunch in public."

To most people that might not sound like a big deal, but if there's one thing Mr. DeVito doesn't take lightly, it's food. Food and insults. I once had the privilege of witnessing him putting a waiter in a chokehold for accidently spilling a bowl of tomato soup on his lap. Needless to say, we were never welcomed back to the restaurant. Chargers were never pressed though. I assume the waiter got a threatening earful from one of the boys.

Mr. DeVito continues to explain. "He lives in a flat over on Fifth Street. Name's Johnson."

I reluctantly take the file and test the weight in my hand. That's the reason I retired. I couldn't take the weight of the jobs anymore.

"Why me? You've got other hit men. What about the guy who just shot the Chief of police? He could pull off this job in his sleep."

"Have you been gone that long? You know I never use the same guy for more than one job in a row. Things get messy if you do that. No, I want you to do this."

What's the point of arguing a losing battle? What the boss wants, the boss gets.

"Any particular methods?"

As if anticipating this question, he replies, "Slowly, painfully and make em' cry." He pulls out his bottom desk drawer and sets an overflowing glass ashtray in front of me. "And dump this in his face. I've been saving up."

I take the ashtray. "I understand, sir."

"Good. Now get out."

Chapter 2

Today is Tuesday. Mr. DeVito expects me to track down, stalk and murder a complete stranger in four days, not counting today since it's already half over.

To be honest, I've had harder jobs with a short time frame. But it's been a few years and I'm a bit rusty.

First things first, if I don't put these ashes in a bag, they're going to fly out.

I head home and after the ashes are sealed up in a plastic bag, I go through the file. Not much is in it. Just a single paper with basic information, name, age, address and race. At least there's a picture of him. He looks wimpy with glasses and a bow tie. Then again, looks can be very deceiving.

I make myself a quick pastrami on rye sandwich before heading over to fifth street to scope out the area.

I find the address and check the names on the mailboxes inside the building. Yup, there's a Johnson who lives here. Apartment 3B. Smack in between Sander in 2B and Brown in 4B I take a stroll up the two flights of stairs. I take note of the window just down the hall and notice that it looks out at Sam's drug store. I find 3B and knock on the door.

I hear some commotion on the other side and it takes a bit for someone to answer. When the door opens, it's a woman and she's got a toddler on her hip and kid clinging to her apron, looking me up and down.

"Can I help you?" she asks tiredly. Her face is flushed and her hair, that might have been in place that morning, is sticking out at crazy ends.

"Perhaps. I'm looking for a Mr. Andrew Johnson. Is he in?"

The toddler starts to fuss and the woman gently bounces him to calm him down. "Andrew is my husband. Who are you? How do you know him?"

I could kick myself for throwing in his first name! I really am rusty. I chuckle lightly to ease her suspicion. A nervous wife will tip off her husband. Which will make my job harder.

61

"I don't exactly know him, ma'am. I'm going door to door, taking surveys about shaving cream. Can you tell me, which brand does your husband prefer?"

The woman studies me carefully, almost buying my seasoned lie. After a moment, she says, "Rayburns." Quickly she adds, "Aren't surveys supposed to be anonymous? Why are you asking for him by name?"

This one is smart. Of course, If I hadn't slipped up… I pretend to jot down the brand as if it's important.

"I'm just following the list, ma'am. And Mr. Andrew Johnson is listed next, followed by Mr. Brown. I'm sorry to have taken up your time. Thank you for your help."

Before she can say anything, I tip my hat respectfully and go next door to the Brown's and knock on the door. A large man, who apparently doesn't even own a razor, answers and tells me to get lost before I can even say hello.

On my way back down, I take another good look out the window in the hall before leaving and walking across the street to Sam's. I can easily judge where their apartment is. From this side of the street I can also get a decent view of the building entrance. I go inside the drug store and take a seat at the counter and order a coffee, black, while I wait for Andrew to come home.

Chapter 3

"I'm telling you, Andrew. He wasn't here about shaving cream. He was here to...to..." Tammy is in hysterics and she has every right to be. She glares at her husband. "Why did you have to get involved with that loan shark? I could have gotten a part time job-"

Andrew doesn't let her finish. "We've been through this, Tammy. You're not getting a job. No woman of mine is working. Besides you've got your hands full with the kids and the house work."

Tammy throws up her hands in disgust. "House work? At a time like this, worry about the house work! Susan from next door can watch the kids. It would only be for a few hours and I can still have your dinner ready..."

"No! Get that idea out of your head right now. Your place is here! And as for that shaving cream fella, I want you to forget him too. He wrote down Rayburn, didn't he?"

"You didn't see him. He looked like...like one of them. The way he carried himself. The devious look in his eye. He's tracking you down, Andrew. I wouldn't be surprised if he waited around outside until you got home."

Andrew sighs. "You've been reading those crime thrillers again, haven't you? Woman, that paperback trash is making you distrustful. What's next? You gonna accuse the postman of poisoning our mail?"

"You wouldn't believe me even if it were true," she says hatefully.

Andrew takes a step forward and slaps her face. "I don't want to hear another word out of you about this. You remember your place and keep your nose out of my affairs."

Tammy fights to keep it together. Crying is a sign of weakness and she isn't about to give him the satisfaction. Andrew storms to the door and grabs his hat and coat.

"Where are you going?" she calls out.

"Out!" He slams the door, making a hanging picture frame fall from its hook.

Chapter 4

It's just after noon on Thursday. After tailing Mr. Johnson to his workplace and scoping out the area yet again, I'm back at Sam's drug store having a chocolate soda at the counter while I wait for him to come home. Another day is coming to a close and if I'm completely honest, I don't know what I'm doing.

I could do a classic hit and run but he always seems to be in a group; walking to and from work and on the job. I did see him go out to the bar the other night. That would have been the ideal opportunity. Too bad I missed it.

"I thought I might find you here." a female voice says as she comes up beside me. I'm hoping its Sandy or Linda. Or even Catherine. I'm surprised to see Mrs. Johnson. She sits next to me and orders a strawberry shake.

"Pardon me?" I ask.

"Don't insult me. Just because I wear a skirt doesn't mean I don't have a brain. You can see the building perfectly from this place and watch him come and go."

The soda jerk places her shake and a straw in front of her. She opens the straw and plops it in the pink beverage.

After taking a long drink, she nonchalantly asks, "Have you decided how you're going to do it?"

This encounter is just too weird. There's no way she could possibly know about…that. "Ma'am? I don't know what you're implying. If you're upset about me bothering you the other day about the survey, I'm truly sorry."

"You've got nothing to gain by lying. It's obvious that you don't know the first thing about pulling off a job like this. Let me help you. I've played out his death in my mind hundreds of times. From poison to suffocation."

There's no doubt now that she knows exactly what my intentions are. To deny it anymore would only cause a scene. "Listen, lady. You might have me figured out but you have no idea what you're getting yourself into."

She laughs lightly. "On the contrary, I've read enough crime thrillers, some of them so gruesome and violent that you can't look at spaghetti sauce the same way." She takes a drink of her shake and adds, "For the record, I know more about your Mr. DeVito than you could imagine. I've been following his bloody trail in the papers for years. That bit with the chief of police had his name written all over it."

I glance over my shoulder nervously. If DeVito heard her talking, she'd be in deep trouble.

"Are you…afraid?" she says tauntingly. "No wonder you can't pull off this simple job." She takes out a compact mirror from her purse and sets it on the counter.

That's it. I can only take so much. I raise a finger to let her have it, but she's standing up. "If you change your mind; you know where to find me. Andrew gets home at five-thirty sharp." She smiles mischievously. "But of course, you knew that already."

I stare at the shake she left on the counter. It isn't even half finished. Beside it is the mirror she left. What was it I was saying earlier about not knowing what I was doing?

The door opens, setting the bells ringing to alert the employees. Mrs. Johnson steps one foot outside. It's now or never.

"Wait, ma'am!" Mrs. Johnson turns, looking as innocent as a newborn despite the fact that she was just talking murder not two minutes ago. Other people in the drug store curiously glance my way and I add, "You forgot this." I pick up the mirror and together we walk out the door and begin to make plans.

Tammy hangs up the phone just as Andrew comes in from work.

"Who was that?" he asks in his usual grouchy way.

"Your mother. She wants the kids to spend the night with her tomorrow. I didn't think you'd mind and I told her I would drop them off after lunch."

Andrew kicks off his shoes and sinks into his favorite chair. "Better my mother than yours." He picks up the evening paper that's waiting for him on the side table and starts to flip through it. No kisses. No, how was your day, honey. No, gee something sure smells good, thanks for slaving over a hot stove all day when it's ninety-five degrees outside. Not even a simple hello or a smile. Tammy thought she would be used to this by now, but with each passing day it grates on her nerves more and more.

Dinner is silent except for the hollow clinking of silverware against his great-grandma's china, and the toddler whining for more milk.

Tammy avoids eye contact with Andrew. They've been married seven years. Aside from the children, they've been the worst years of her life. Andrew is constantly abusing her, both physically and mentally. Tammy feels worthless, unappreciated and unloved.

If there was any way to finally put this miserable marriage out of its misery, it was tomorrow. She reaches into her apron pocket and fingers the tiny glass vile.

Just a little bit of rattlesnake venom should do the trick. She resists the urge to smile and instead offers Andrew another slice of meatloaf.

Chapter 5

I can't believe I actually went through with this deal of Tammy's. I must have been more desperate than I thought. Never before have I ever worked with someone on a job, let alone a woman. I need to remember never to get on her bad side.

When she first told me that I need to get her some rattlesnake venom, I thought she was crazy. But then she explained that Andrew uses a straight razor and not a morning goes by that he doesn't cut himself on the first stroke. Tammy said she would put some venom on his razor and the job should finish itself. By lunchtime at the earliest, it should take effect and everyone will think he's suffering a heart attack. Conveniently, he has high blood pressure and has been on pills for it for a long time.

It should be a slow and painful death, just as DeVito ordered, minus the ashtray. There's no way I can pull that off.

But will it work? I hate not doing this sort of the thing the traditional way. I'm used to having my hands all over the scene, either gunning them down or sticking a knife to 'em. This sneaky tactic is too unnerving. Too modern for my taste. Give me a good old trusty machine gun any day.

As for the snake venom, it was easy to get. You just need to know the right people, which I do.

I glance at the clock on the wall of Sam's drug store. It's almost noon. Tammy should be at her mother in-law's, dropping the kids off. This gives her an alibi, just in case the cops start to think outside the box of natural causes. As for my alibi, I ordered four cheese burgers without the buns. With a strange order like this, I won't soon be forgotten.

We agreed it would be wisest not to meet after this. If the plan works, she'll let me know by leaving an old-fashioned black wreath on her apartment door by tomorrow, Saturday. The wreath is a sign of mourning. If there's no wreath, then I'll have to pull this off by myself. And fast.

Here comes my lunch. I settle down to enjoy my alibi and make myself as memorable as I can without being asked to leave.

Two days later, on Sunday, I find myself once again sitting in Mr. DeVito's office as he reads aloud from the morning paper:

"Worst Heart Attack Ever Witnessed: Mr. Johnson, former employee at a local brewing company, suffered a terrible heart attack yesterday just after lunch. Witnesses say it was a dreadful ordeal and he screamed as if he were being repeatedly stabbed with a blunt knife. Authorities agree that Mr. Johnson's inaccurate high blood pressure medicine is possibly to blame and police are currently investigating."

Mr. DeVito rolls the paper up tightly and smacks the desk top with it. "Music to my ears. I don't know how you pulled it off, Steve, but this is gold. How'd you do it? How'd you make it look like a heart real attack?"

I chuckle and scratch at the scruff on my chin. "You know what they say, a magician doesn't give away trade secrets."

DeVito isn't happy with this answer but doesn't fight it. "I just wish you would have dumped the ashes on him. Like I told you to do."

"I still have the ashes, if you want to wait a week or two and do the honors yourself."

"*Myself?* Vinny DeVito didn't get to where he is today by *doing the honors himself.* Now you just leave this office the way you came in and do the honors yourself!"

I hide a smile as I leave. As I pass Linda's desk, I ask her out to dinner after her shift is over, to which she accepts. All the while, DeVito is still fuming in his office, appalled that it was even suggested that he do his own dirty work for once.

Epilogue

As for Tammy, she and the kids moved in with her mother. Tammy got a job working in a clothing shop, making a decent living and enjoying her freedom. During the evenings she worked tirelessly on her very own murder mystery novella entitled, Venom. It became an overnight best seller and she went on to publish over forty crime books, all with equal massive success. She remained single and lived a long and happy life.

The Eternal Shining Star

Chapter 1

"I don't wish to see anyone! Can't an old woman live out her last days in peace?"

"But Ms. Smith, it will do you good to have company."

"Pah! I don't want any company. Send whoever it is away!"

Mrs. Paul, a nurse at the Fischer retirement center, opens the automatic door and wheels out a very perturbed eighty-nine-year-old woman in to the sitting room. She's ready to protest when she sees her 'company'.

Sitting alone on a rickety wooden chair is a girl. She can't be any older than thirteen. She's staring at the old woman, no doubt having heard every word and feeling uncomfortable at the prospect of meeting her.

Mrs. Paul begins the introductions. "Ms. Smith, this is Jami Williams. Jami, this is Ms. Sandra Smith. I'll leave you two alone to get acquainted. Ring the bell on the desk if either of you need anything."

Ms. Smith's initial surprise at seeing Jami has passed is replaced with her usual suspicion.

"Let's have it out then. What do you want from me? If it's money, I don't have a dime to my name. If it's an autograph, I have arthritis. If it's an interview you're after, I won't give you a single word. You may be young but I've had enough dealings with journalists to know how it works. I'll not have my good name smeared through the rubbish and you can quote me on that."

Jami's mouth is open but no words come. She can't tear her gaze from the woman's glitzy sleeveless evening gown. Or the gloves that go up past her boney elbows. Not to mention the layers of pearl necklaces draped around her neck and the diamond earrings that make her lobes droop. And there's her make up that she must have done herself with an unsteady hand. The eyeliner travels up and down like a line on heart monitor. Her false black eyelashes stick out like angry spiders. Most noticeable are the bright red circles of rouge on her cheeks.

Ms. Smith feels as if she's being silently judged. "Ah! Come to gawk, have you? Come to stare at the remains of a bygone era? Well I don't have to put up with this."

She begins to wheel herself away when Jami finds her voice.

"No, I'm only here for my community service hours for school. Honest."

Ms. Smith sneers. "That's all? You're just here for a grade and not to see *me*? I should have known."

"You said something about autographs? Are you, I mean; were you an actress or something?"

Ms. Smith squints in confusion. "You mean to say, you don't know who I am?"

Jami shakes her head.

"I'm Sandra Smith!"

Jami shifts in her seat, feeling uncomfortable. "Sorry, but I don't know you. I just asked to see a resident who doesn't get any visitors."

That was the wrong thing to say. Jami realizes this after it's too late. The woman's pride has taken a hard blow but she pretends as if it didn't sting.

78

"In that case, allow me to enlighten you. I was once known as the Queen of the Silver Screen. I was in several pictures, received rave reviews from critics and won many awards for best actress." She pauses, the fire in her eyes fading. "I see none of that matters now."

"I had no idea you were actually *somebody*," Jami says in surprise.

Ms. Smith frowns. "Jami, is it? Jami, *everybody* is a *somebody*. You make it sound like I'm some sort of extraterrestrial."

"Tell me what it was like," Jami asks, partly out of pure curiosity and partly to the watch the glimmer of magic light up in the woman's eyes again. She might be up in years, but age hasn't diminished the power of her stage presence.

Ms. Smith wants to but is cautious. "You really want to know?"

"Yes. I just joined the theater club at school and I really like it."

Ms. Smith scoffs. "If it's acting tips you want, you can forget that too. You can take all the acting, singing and dancing lessons there are. You can hire the best trainers and instructors that money can buy. Routines, lines and songs can be memorized until you can do them in your sleep. But talent, raw, God-given talent is something you either have or you don't have and no amount of money or time spent can ever acquire it."

Jami nods, mesmerized by the woman's brutally honest words. "How did you get your start?"

"My grandfather was one of the great actors of the silent film era. When talkies came in fashion, he was luckier than most because he had a nice voice. He always told me that talkies were the ruin of the entertainment business. The world lost a lot of good talent just because their voice wasn't what the studio had in mind.

"He was always taking me on set when I was a little girl. I instantly fell in love with the movies and wanted to be a part of the magic. My father, on the other hand, worked as a grocer and forbid me from following in his father's career.

"I'll never forget the date. December 13th 1943. I had the lead in a play at the local theater. Little did I know, my grandfather invited Mr. Selmer, a friend and producer, to

80

come and watch me perform. Mr. Selmer later told me that when he saw me up on stage, it was like no one else mattered. I had the audience eating out of the palm of my hand, hanging onto my every word. Before Christmas I was signed on with the studio and was given a minor part in a film starring some of the biggest names in that day. The rest is history."

Jami is sitting on the edge of her seat. "I bet your dad was furious!"

"Oh, furious doesn't begin to cut it. In fact, he cut me from his will. It was years before I saw him again. By then he was a crippled old man."

"What about your mom?"

"My mother died in childbirth with my baby brother. He was stillborn."

"I'm sorry, Ms. Smith."

"What's to be sorry about? Any amount of condolences isn't going to change anything." She cleared her throat, ready to change the subject. "Are you going to make an old woman carry the conversation or were you going to contribute something?"

Jami tilts her head. "What?"

"You know more about me that I even intended to tell and all I know about you besides your name is that you're only here for a grade. I find myself in a very unfair disadvantage. Tell me about you."

"Oh." Jami quickly tries to think of something exciting to share but nothing comes to mind. "There's not much to say about me. I'm fourteen and I go to Lincoln Middle school. I'm an only child and I'm a vegetarian."

Ms. Smith chuckles. "That will do. Tell me more about this community service project."

"Everyone's supposed to volunteer or do something in the community for three hours."

Ms. Smith doesn't like the sound of this. "You expect me to sit in this horrible chair for three hours? I would barely have time to freshen up before bingo and there's my nap to consider."

Jami smiles and hurries to explain. "No, not three hours straight. I was thinking an hour a day, if that's alright with you."

"Three days?" She considers this. "Why, of all the great things you could do for the community, did you choose to visit an old cranky bat like me?"

Jami doesn't answer right away because she knows her reasoning probably sounds ridiculous.

"Let's just say that I have a personal reason for doing this and leave it at that."

The woman nods, respecting the straight forward answer. "Alright. How much longer for today?"

Jami checks the stopwatch on her phone. "About thirty-two minutes. We don't have to just talk. There's a chess board over there if you want to play."

"Chess? What do you take me for? A battle strategist? Heavens no! However, I am fond of cards. Do you play poker?"

Over the next half hour, Ms. Smith teaches Jami the basics of poker. It takes a few hands before Jami begins to catch on. During the final hand, Jami even wins.

"Jami?"

Jami turns and sees Mrs. Paul standing behind her, smiling at the scene. It warms her heart to see Sandra enjoying herself.

"Yes?" Jami asks.

"I believe it's time for Ms. Smith's nap," Mrs. Paul states gently.

"A nap? Who has time for a nap?" Ms. Smith argues. "If I were a gambler, I'd have taken this girl for every penny."

Jami smiles. "Except for that last hand. Do you mind if I come back tomorrow? Same time?"

Ms. Smith sighs. "You're determined to pester me, aren't you? If you must bother me tomorrow, bring paper and pencil. If you're as interested in my life as you seem, I'll give you a list of the pictures I was in."

Jami says her goodbyes and thanks Ms. Smith for her time. In return, the woman flashes a smile that thousands of cameras have captured and cherished.

Chapter 2

Over the course of the next few months, Jami became a constant presence at the retirement center. Her community service hours were long ago fulfilled but neither she nor Sandra ever mentioned this.

Every day after school they would spend the allotted hour talking about Sandra's movies, favorite scenes, and fellow actors and actress.

During one particular meeting, Sandra informed Jami that there was a vast difference between her personal favorite film and the film she's most known for. While her most popular film, The Scarlet Thread, was her first big break and gave her a large following, Sandra admitted that she felt the story was lacking and her co-stars were less than friendly toward her.

Her favorite film to work on was called, Water lilies in the Ocean, a heartfelt drama with a good amount of comic relief. The entire experience was a pleasure and she made a lot of lifelong friendships during it.

When they weren't talking movies, they played poker, gin rummy, and checkers, which Sandra insisted wasn't a game of strategy, but rather a game of luck.

Jami rarely talked about her home life or school. She thought her life was dull and boring compared to the life of an actress. However, Sandra showed subtle interest in Jami's life. She would ask questions such as, "What does this new generation do for entertainment?" or, "What are they teaching you youngsters in school nowadays?"

One of Jami's most memorable conversations went like this:

"Did you ever have to play a character that you hated?" Jami inquired.

Sandra didn't need to consider the question for long. "A true actress becomes their character. She learns to talk, walk, and think like her character to achieve the believability that we all strive for. It's one thing to disagree with your character's beliefs or personality. But to say I *hate* my character is to say that I hate myself. And if there's one thing I learned in show biz, it's to always love yourself because there's always someone ready to tear you down. However, there was one particular role in which the dialogue was simply dreadful. I adlibbed most of my lines." She gave a conspiratorial grin. "This infuriated the director, of course."

Jami loved to watch Sandra talk about the picture making business. It was like something buried deep inside the woman came to life every time. Her eyes sparkled with wonder and she became very animated. Jami could listen to her for hours, entranced by Sandra's gift for storytelling.

Little did Jami realize how much of a positive impact she was making on Sandra. Having a visitor gave her something she hadn't realized she'd missed after all these years- friendship. A single hour with Jami gave Sandra a reason to wake up each day, despite the aches and pains. Not only was her health improving little by little, but her overall mood and morale as well. Mrs. Paul especially noticed the change.

However, Jami's parents lacked the same enthusiasm that everyone else had. They'd encouraged Jami in the beginning and thought her idea to visit a lonely patient in a retirement center was very noble and kind gesture. But overtime they grew concerned that their daughter was spending *too* much time there and needed to spend more time with people her own age. Despite several hints to this, Jami continued to visit Sandra without fail.

The months flew by and, what started as an awkward meeting, bloomed into an unexpected friendship.

Chapter 3

Today is the last day of school and Jami is at the center a little earlier than usual because school let out early.

Jami had been anticipating a lazy summer spent at the nursing home until her parents confronted her that morning before school and informed her that they are leaving in three days and spending the majority of the summer traveling along the historic route sixty-six.

Jami walks up the familiar sidewalk to the entrance and opens the door. She is well-known at the retirement center and is often greeted on a first name bases with a handful of the residents and workers.

She signs her name on the guest sheet and takes a seat in the lobby to wait for Sandra. Sometimes Sandra is already there and will say something to the effect of, "What took you so long? Ask anyone, time is money."

Today the lobby is empty. There isn't even a nurse at the front desk. Jami waits a little longer before deciding to head to Sandra's room to check on her.

Jami had been in Sandra's room on two occasions. One was when Sandra asked her to fetch something from the room, an emerald ring she'd forgotten to put on that morning, and another when Sandra wasn't feeling strong enough to sit in her wheelchair. They'd spent the hour that day pouring over what Sandra liked to call her treasures. Newspaper clippings, playbills from her stage performances. She even kept a napkin from one of her first important dinner parties. In marker, she'd written across the bottom: Friday, April 12th 1944.

Stepping foot inside Sandra's room was like stepping back in time. It was amazing how much memorabilia and tokens Sandra had held onto over the years. From original movie posters, old time photos, and handwritten letters and notes from stars long gone.

Unarguably, the most impressive item was stored in a plastic bag in the back of the closet. The iconic red dress she'd worn in, The Scarlet Thread. After filming was complete, Sandra bought the dress and kept it all these years. It was still in mint condition. It wasn't a well-known fact that she had the dress.

She'd explained to Jami that day she'd brought it out from the closet, "If people knew I had this, I'd never have a moment's piece again. That dress is worth millions today and a collector would gladly give their right arm for it."

As Jami comes to Sandra's room, she finds the door ajar and knocks as she slowly pushes it open, revealing an empty and sad room

The bed is vacant. The sheets are gone. There's not a sight of any of Sandra's personal belongings.

Someone else enters the room.

"Jami? I wasn't expecting you for at least another hour," Mrs. Paul says.

Jami is glad to finally see a familiar face but feels alarm rising up inside her. "Where's Sandra? Has she been moved to a different room?" That would be a reasonable explanation.

Mrs. Paul sadly shakes her head, wishing she could spare Jami the hurt she's going to feel. "No, my dear. Sandra passed away in her sleep late last night, peaceful as anything. I'm sorry, Jami. If it helps at all, she wasn't in any pain when she went."

The words are a jumble that Jami can't quite unscramble. Dead? She can't be dead! She was so full of life.

"But I just saw her yesterday!" Jami argues, fighting back tears.

Mrs. Paul nods in agreement. "I know. It came as a shock to all of us. Based on her recent charts, she could have lived at least another seven years, possibly more. But the Lord had other plans. She lived a full and beautiful life."

A tear runs down Jami's check and she angrily brushes it away. "It's not fair! Why did she have to go?"

Mrs. Paul gives Jami a hug. "You have no idea the impact you made in her life. She's told me more than once after you left, "Don't let me oversleep tomorrow. I don't want to be late for our visit." Mrs. Paul pulls away, suddenly remembering something. "I have something for you. Wait here and I'll be right back."

Jami doesn't have to wait long. Mrs. Paul returns carrying a medium sized cardboard box. When Jami doesn't move to take the box, Miss Paul sets it on the floor. "Ms. Smith was going through her belongings the other day, shortly before you arrived. She wanted you to have these. There's more too, tucked safely away in a storage closet. She told me, before her nap that same day, to give everything she had to you. Her first real friend she's had in a long, long time."

Jami feels sick to her stomach. "I can't take all her stuff. Doesn't she have family?"

"No. She had no one. Except for you."

Jami moves as if in a blur. She picks up the box and tells Mrs. Paul that she'll be back later with her parents to collect everything else. She says a numb goodbye and leaves the Fischer's retirement center for one of the last times.

That evening, after everything is said and done and the devastating news has plenty of time to fully sink in, Jami sits on the couch with her parents and they watch Water lilies in the Ocean. The box contained all of Sandra's treasures. In the back of Jami's closet, hangs the iconic red dress safely protected in the plastic bag.

The family watches as the beautiful Sandra Smith, full of life and energy, acts, and sings on T.V. Jami watches Sandra's eyes during the frequent close ups for the magic that so sparkled and captivated. She is not disappointed.

Too quickly, the movie ends. The silver screen flickers and it's over.

The star is gone but not forgotten.

End

The Diamond Eye Boutique

Chapter 1

"I'll be back in a minute; I just want to try on this top," Hannah told her friends.

"Well, hurry up. We want to go have lunch!" Samantha replied in her usual nagging tone.

Hannah waved her friends off and hurried to the women's fitting room. Inside, she took in her surroundings, impressed with what she saw. Plush red carpet from wall to wall, a dozen overly-spacious fitting rooms with golden knobs, a wraparound leather couch that hugged the far corner and two brightly lit three-way mirrors on either side of the room.

"Wow! Now *this* is what I call a fitting room!" Hannah said with a smile.

The Diamond Eye Boutique was extremely lavish and high class. They only sold name brand products but surprisingly, the prices were rather reasonable- some products were priced at less than half of what the item would normally sell for. Today was their grand opening and there was a steady stream of excited shoppers coming and going in droves all day.

Hannah opened the nearest fitting room and stepped inside.

Twenty minutes later...

"That's it! I'm going in there and I'm dragging her out by her hair!" Samantha exclaimed as she stomped off towards the fitting room.

Ashley looked down anxiously at her phone for the hundredth time. "She hasn't answered any of the calls or texts. Do you think something happened to her? It shouldn't take her this long to try on one shirt."

Dorothy gave a short laugh, trying to lighten the mood. "You know Hannah. She's probably going through all of the clothes on the return racks and trying them on too."

"But she's always good about answering her phone. I'm getting really scared," Ashley insisted.

Suddenly Samantha came hurrying back and looked around nervously.

"What's wrong? Where's Hannah?" asked Ashley.

Samantha switched her gaze between her friends and the surrounding area. "Did you guys see her come out?"

"No. What's going on?" demanded Dorothy. Samantha's attitude was worrying both of them.

Samantha looked back in the direction of the fitting room and shrugged helplessly. "I don't know. Hannah's just…gone."

Chapter 2

"Grand opening Gag. Reports from the recently opened Diamond Eye Boutique tell of an odd disappearance of sixteen-year-old girl, Hannah Newman. Authorities confirm the account as nothing more than a *prank*."

George Newman slammed the newspaper down on the polished Mahogany desk of Officer McCain.

"If it's just a prank then tell me where my daughter is!" Hannah's father exclaimed.

Mr. Newman's fiery glare would be enough to intimidate most, but Officer McCain had received his share of scowls and glares from belligerent criminals that he was unmoved. But Mr. Newman was not a criminal. He was an angry and frightened parent who just wanted answers. What he needed now was a calm voice of reason.

Officer McCain nodded, to show that he wasn't just listening, but understood. "I fully understand that, sir. Prank or not, Hannah is still missing. The papers should have never printed that story. Have a seat and I'll explain where I'm at in the case."

Mr. Newman complied and the officer began.

"After we received a call from Ashley Roberts, a friend of Hannah, alerting us that Hannah was missing, we did a thorough investigation of the store, focusing mainly on the last place Hannah was seen. This search came up empty. We didn't find any evidence of a struggle. None of Hannah's personal belongings were found. Our forensic team didn't find any of Hannah's DNA at scene either.

"I personally checked the security tapes and at the time of Hannah's disappearance, no one was seen entering or leaving the fitting room. To be perfectly clear, there was no proof that Hannah had even been *in* the boutique. All we really have to go on is the word of Hannah's friends."

Mr. Newman's expression darkened. "What exactly are you implying?"

"I'm not trying to imply anything. According to the facts, Hannah was never there." He paused before adding, "This may be hard to consider, but did you and your daughter have any problems at home? Major disagreements or arguments?"

"You think that I did something to Hannah?" Mr. Newman interrupted angrily, rising to his feet.

"No, your alibi at the BMV checks out. I was referring to the possibility that Hannah ran away," McCain calmly explained. "She could have easily talked her friends into helping her. It's not unheard of."

George collapsed back in his seat and held his head in his hands.

"Maybe she did run away. I never said the right things to her. After her mom passed away, I tried to be both mother and father but I couldn't."

"Mr. Newman, don't blame yourself."

After a moment, Mr. Newman let out a heavy sigh. "What do I do now? If she really did run away how do I get her back?"

"That's what we're working on now. We sent out alerts and were trying to look into where she might have gone or who she might be staying with."

Mr. Newman shrugged, distressed and at a loss. "I'm all she had when it came to family."

101

"What about a location?" The officer pressed. "Where there any places that were special to her? Any that she talked about?"

Mr. Newman shook his head. "Hannah never told me anything. There was always a barrier between us when it came to communication. It's hard telling where she'd go."

Knowing that there was nothing else he could glean from the conversation, Officer McCain said, "I'm sorry you have to deal with this. I want you to know that we are working on this case and we'll keep you informed on any updates. Likewise, please call if you remember any information that might be of help."

Mr. Newman nodded. The men shook hands and Mr. Newman left, feeling discouraged and defeated.

Chapter 3

Over the course of the next two weeks, there were seven more similar missing-persons cases that took place inside the Diamond Eye Boutique but they all deferred in details, including age, race, gender and locations within the store.

The local papers didn't miss a beat and gleefully reported each one: Betty Sands, age fifty-two. Crystal Mutton, age seven. Zach Trust, age twenty-eight. Regina Yetts, age thirty-four. Jacob Myall, age ten. Raymond Cutler, age sixty. Quinton Reynolds, age nineteen.

Officer McCain felt personally responsible for basically blowing off Hannah's disappearance and was determined to make things right. Focusing all his time and energy into the strange disappearances, he began a full-fledged private investigation.

One of the first things he looked into was a possible connection and all that he came up with was the boutique. It might sound feasible for a teenager to run off and use her friends to help pull off the stunt, but it was unrealistic that all of these individuals would do the same.

Mrs. Sands, for example, was a proud grandma of four who was due to embark on a cruise in one week. Her husband said she was out shopping for some last-minute items for the trip and never came home. Oddly enough, the security cameras never showed her arrive at the boutique but her car was in the parking lot. All the facts pointed to the conclusion that she'd just left her house one day and vanished without a trace. This, of course, couldn't be right.

And there was Crystal Mutton, the youngest of the victims. Her mother claimed to have turned her back for two minutes while Crystal was getting a drink at the water fountain. Next thing she knew Crystal was gone.

There was definitely something fishy going on at the boutique and Officer McCain wasn't going to rest until he had some answers.

Pulling up in the deserted parking lot, he exited his car and headed to the boutique entrance. Crossing over the police tape, he made his way inside. After a total of eight disappearances within two weeks, the once eager shoppers were now leery to come near the place. It was cheaper to temporary close down the shop than to stay open for the one or two brave bargain-hunters who still faithfully shopped. While it was bad for business, it certainly helped with the investigation.

The frustrating part was that he didn't know exactly what he was looking for. The most recent case, Quinton Reynolds, had taken place just yesterday in the young men's department. A team was currently crowded in the department taking pictures and gathering any and all evidence.

McCain shook his head disdainfully as he looked on at the chaos. *It will be just like the others. Don't waste your time.*

Walking to the opposite side of the store, he passed by the stockroom that was blocked by crime scene tape. The stockroom had already been searched, but it never hurt to try again.

Turning the knob, he found it was locked. This didn't strike him as unusual and he was ready to move on when he caught sight of something through the small square window.

Doing a double take, he saw it was only a store mannequin. Nothing strange about that.

He frowned, a new thought occurring to him. Not once had he ever seen a mannequin in the store. Yet, there was one in the stockroom?

Without any delay, he obtained a master key from a fellow officer and began his own search. It seemed like an ordinary stockroom. Racks of clothes were ready for display. Shelves contained box upon box of merchandise. But the mannequin that had caught his attention...was gone.

In the back of the room, was a door that was slightly open. McCain moved cautiously, the hairs on the back of his neck stood on end. Opening the door, the rest of the way, he came face to face with not one, but eight store mannequins all huddling together, including the one that had been in the other room. Four females and four males, varying in size and shape. Although they were made of plastic, they had a lifelike quality about them. Eight pair of eyes stared back at him.

Fear tugged at his heart. "There's no way. It's all a coincidence. It has to be. But it would explain a lot..." he shook these absurd

106

thoughts away. People can't turn into mannequins. *But how did that one mannequin get in here? There's no one else in here but me...*

On an impulse he came to a decision. Borrowing a camera from another officer, he took pictures of the mannequins. Then one by one, he took all the mannequins out of the storeroom. He wasn't sure how he could use them in the case, but this was the first solid piece of evidence since the first disappearance. Besides, leaving them locked away somehow seemed cruel.

Chapter 4

Not long after Officer McCain confiscated the mannequins as evidence, Veronica Mills, the owner of the Diamond Eye Boutique, sued him for theft, claiming he stole private property and he had no right to be in the stockroom to begin with.

The papers ate this up and soon it was all anyone was talking about. The majority of the town did admit that the connections between the store mannequins and the missing people were eerily on point, but no one was willing to go as far to claim what was secretly at the back of everyone's mind.

During the trial, this theory was brought up several times and when questioned about it, Veronica laughed it off as being ridiculous and called the local law enforcement, a lot of superstitious women.

When asked why the mannequins had been locked away in the storeroom instead of out on the sales floor, she explained that she made her own mannequins, a hobby of hers, and they weren't ready for display yet. This, and all her other reasonable answers and explanations, made Officer McCain and his theory look foolish. Of course, no one believed his encounter with the mannequin who moved from room to room on its own and he had no way to prove it.

In the end, Veronica won back her mannequins and graciously accepted Officer McCain's public apology, her only condition aside from the return of her property.

McCain was angry with whole affair, the apology being the final straw. After a considerable amount of research on Veronica, nothing came up. She was either using a fake identity or...something. He didn't know how to explain it or prove it, but he believed wholeheartedly that somehow those missing people were the mannequins. There were just too many creepy coincidences to ignore.

Watching Veronica take back her "property" made him sick. Like watching a kidnapper reclaim their victim. The depressing part was that the families still held unto the hope that maybe they would be reunited with their loved ones someday, a hope McCain knew was pointless.

Oddly enough, as soon as the store closed down for good, the disappearances came to an abrupt end. Offended with her tarnished reputation, Veronica packed up and moved away, taking the mannequins with her.

Shortly after, Officer McCain retired from law enforcement. He spent the rest his days silently following Veronica's trail of new stores and the strange disappearances that came with them, hoping somehow to bust the cases wide open. Unfortunately, this was an unfulfilled dream.

After several years, the total number of missing people added up to eighty-eight. Eleven boutiques. Eight victims every time. Four males. Four females.

Simply coincidence? Or something else entirely different?

End

Starlight

The blank sky overhead was dark and empty. The summer air was warm; perfect for sitting outside.

That's where Emma was that night, as she sat on the grass of her front yard. The smell of freshly cut grass hung in the air from that afternoon. Looking upward, she felt small beneath the immense sky as it looked down at her. The blades of grass tickled her legs but she didn't mind as she anticipated the show that was about to begin.

Suddenly, she saw it. The first star. Far off in the distance a bright twinkle of light appeared. It flickered and danced as it stood alone in the blackness. Then a second star took the stage. It gleamed brightly as it preformed its own delicate dance.

One by one, more stars appeared against the rich velvet sky. Individually, they were small, but together, they overpowered the darkness.

Emma smiled as she gazed upward. The show was mesmerizing and she was entranced by its magic. Before long the sky was overflowing with its diamonds, too innumerable to count.

The time passed swiftly and before she knew it, it was time to go back inside. The stars took a bow and watched as their audience of one stood and made her way inside her home.

The stars turned their attention to another part of the wide world and began their show once more, for anyone willing to take the time to simply look up.

End

Friendship is Stronger

Chapter 1

Sarah carefully placed her cell phone on the table. A lump was in her throat. Her emotions jumped from one extreme to the other. Disbelief, fear, despair, concern, anger, and the current one, indignation. It wasn't fair. This happened to other people, complete strangers, but not me! Then she felt horrible for wishing her predicament on someone else instead of her.

Sarah couldn't even remember what she'd been doing before the phone rang. Although it was only a few minutes ago, life seemed different somehow.

At that moment, her phone lit up and obnoxiously vibrated. It was Katie, her friend, calling.

At first Sarah wondered why Katie was calling and then it dawned on her that today was July first. It was a tradition she and her friends came up with to begin their Christmas shopping today, followed by a cookout and a wrapping party at one of their homes. Katie was probably calling to see if she was almost ready to go.

How could she participate in such a joyous occasion now? She knew she would just bring down the mood and ruin it for everyone else.

Sarah picked up the phone to answer, but set it down again. She didn't feel like talking to anyone. What excuse would she give? There was always the truth, but then that would spoil their fun.

The call ended and Sarah put the phone on silent. Sarah grabbed the bag of sour cream and onion chips and munched on a number of them before deciding to crawl in bed for the night.

She didn't get far when there was a knock on the door, followed by a muffled voice, "Sarah? It's me, Katie. Are you alright?"

A phone call was one thing, but how could she ignore this? Katie and the others were probably waiting for her in the driveway. Sarah took a deep breath, plastered on a fake smile and opened the door.

Katie smiled with relief. "Hey, I was getting a little worried. Are you okay?"

Katie was the overprotective, motherly one in their tightly woven friendship, ready to defend and avenge. She was also very observant and had a wild imagination. Katie worked as a receptionist at a doctor's office.

Am I that transparent? Sarah thought with annoyance. "I'm fine, why do you ask?"

"Well…you didn't answer my texts or call, which you always do."

"Maybe I was away from my phone. I'm not attached to it, you know?"

Sarah's snappy remark wasn't lost on Katie and she filed it away in the back of her mind. "So, are you ready to go? The girls are waiting in the car."

Sarah picked at the paint on the door frame. "I'm just going to stay in today. You and the girls go ahead and have fun." She thought this would be a good enough answer but she should have known better.

Katie frowned. "What's wrong, Sarah?"

"I'm just not feeling very good. Don't worry about me. A good night's sleep is all I need."

From the end of the driveway, Katie's car was running patiently. The passenger door opened and a girl waved at them and called,

"What's the hold up? We going shopping or not?"

It was Margaret. Every group of friends has at least one loud, unfiltered friend. Margaret was the friend in this case. She had a talent for saying what was on everyone's mind, despite the repercussions. Outspoken and bold, she was very into politics and instead of a hello or how are you, she often started conversations with phrase such as, did you hear what so-and-so said in last night's press meeting? or, it shouldn't have taken a full-fledged investigation and millions of tax payer dollars to know that so-and-so was a corrupt governor.

Sarah sighed. "Please go on without me. I won't be much fun anyway."

It took some doing but Katie finally relented and the girls left. Sarah watched from the window to make sure they really gone before taking her chips and going to bed to have a pity-party.

Chapter 2

Hours later, a delicious smell woke her from a fitful sleep. Sarah opened her eyes and to her surprise, her friends were sitting around on the floor. A table cloth was spread out and it was covered with a feast of fast food.

"About time! Everything was getting cold," stated Margaret.

"It wouldn't take but a minute to heat it all up in the microwave," suggested Rachel. To Sarah, she said, "I hope you don't mind us surprising you like this. We used the spare key in the flower pot."

Rachel was the positive and happy one in the group. The glass half- full type even if the glass was bone dry. Margaret called her naive. Katie called her a blessing. Rachel was also artistic. She loved drawing and painting. As a self-employed painter, she made a decent living taking requests and selling her own paintings.

Sarah sat up in bed, wide awake now. "How did the shopping go?"

"We didn't go. It wouldn't have been any fun without you," answered Katie.

Sarah crawled out of bed and took a seat between Katie and Rachel. "Wow guys. This is really nice. You did all this for me?"

"No, it's just for us and you get to watch us eat," Margaret teased.

"Really, Margaret. It's clearly obvious that Sarah's in the middle of a life-altering crisis. This is not the time to make senseless remarks," replied Tonya.

Smart, logical, wise beyond her years, Tonya. Always ready with an answer, an explanation, or a theory. Tonya worked in a library by day and a bookstore by night. She spent her weekends reading, drinking tea, posting useless facts on social media and cuddling her cats.

Sarah felt her face grow warm from embarrassment. *Why does everyone assume there's something wrong with me?*

"What makes you say that?" she shot back. "Is it a crime to forgo an afternoon of shopping?"

"Not at all. However, you've displayed several signs that are, how you say, concerning. Isolation, social withdrawal, short-temperedness, and defensiveness. Experts will agree that these signs point to a mid-life crisis. Which is deeply intriguing considering that you're not yet thirty years of age."

Katie took Sarah's hand and softly explained, "Sarah, we know something's wrong. We're your best friends. You can talk to us. Whatever it is, we can get through it together."

"Things usually seem worse when we can't see the big picture. Maybe a different perspective will help," added Rachel.

Sarah couldn't hold the truth back a moment longer. "This afternoon, before you came, I got a call from my doctor. I have cancer."

"Oh, Sarah," Katie breathed out.

Suddenly Rachel reached over and embraced Sarah tightly. Katie, Margaret and Tonya followed and Sarah found herself in a warm embrace.

For the first time since receiving the news, Sarah began to cry. Her friends cried with her and comforted her the best they knew how. Slowly, the hug ended but the love and friendship still surrounded Sarah.

Tonya took off her glasses and wiped the lens on her shirt. "What kind of cancer and what stage?"

"It's some kind of skin cancer but I don't remember what he said. He did say that they caught it early and the surgery shouldn't be difficult at all."

"When's your appointment for the surgery? Did you make one yet?" Katie questioned.

"This coming Wednesday at nine."

"Hope you don't mind having your own personal cheering squad there," Rachel said. "I don't know about you guys, but I'll be there."

"I'd like to see someone try to make us stay away," Margaret added.

Katie nodded. "We're here for you, Sarah."

Tonya had a thoughtful expression and anyone who knew her well enough, could tell she was plotting and planning. "I wouldn't mind speaking with this doctor concerning the surgery. Perhaps I can be a silent observer and take notes during it? You wouldn't mind, would you Sarah?"

Sarah chuckled, feeling much better. "We'll worry about that later."

"Let's quit talking and starting eating. Fast food tastes awful cold," Margret blurted as she popped a fry in her mouth. "Yep, tastes awful."

Chapter 3

Wednesday finally came and at nine that morning, Sarah was prepped for surgery and just waiting for the doctor.

As promised, her friends were there. They took up a small corner in the waiting room with balloons and a large painted sign that exclaimed, "We Love You, Sarah!"

Much to Tonya's dismay, she was not allowed to be a silent observer during the operation.

Almost three hours later, the surgery was a success and she was good to go.

That evening, the group celebrated by ordering in a pizza and having a chick-flick movie marathon.

While Margaret and Tonya were debating over which movie to start with, Katie noticed that something was bothering Sarah.

"You okay?" she asked. "You haven't touched your pizza."

Sarah shrugged and fingered the rim of her plastic cup. "I don't know. I just feel kind of ashamed of myself."

"What's there to ashamed of? I thought you would be happy that everything went well."

"That's just it. Three hours in surgery and it's like nothing even happened. There are some people who don't find out about cancer until it's too late and they have to go on chemo and all sorts of treatments. But they're so strong and brave. What did I do over? I heard the word cancer and I freaked out and had a pity party over something so small and insignificant. I guess I'm not as strong as I'd thought I was."

The room was silent. Margaret and Tonya had stopped arguing and were listening intently.

Katie shook her head. "Listen to me. *Any* kind of cancer, no matter the stage or how deadly, is scary. Do you honestly believe that all cancer patients are able to be strong twenty-four seven? Do you think they don't have moments of weakness? Moments where they just break down and ask, why me? Believe me, Sarah. You were strong. And if you didn't feel like you were carrying all the weight on your shoulders, it's because we were right there with you, carrying the load together."

"That was beautiful," Rachel breathed.

"And I meant every word of it. Now in the words of a very unfiltered friend of mine, let's quit talking and start eating. You know what they say about cold food."

Sarah and Katie exchanged smiles.

"Even though we missed the first, do you guys think we can still carry out our July Christmas shopping tradition this Saturday?"

Margaret gave a doubtful expression. "Gee…I don't know. Next week I was going to start working on my Easter shopping."

Tonya rolled her eyes, not one for sarcasm.

"We wouldn't miss it," Katie answered

End

I'll be Home

Chapter 1

1942~ World War II ~ Christmas Eve.

Doris Allen was busy at work in her kitchen, preparing for tomorrow's dinner. Cheerful Christmas music was blaring from the radio in the living room and Doris was singing along. Christmas was always her favorite time of year.

She had just pulled out the last batch of gingerbread from the oven when the doorbell rang. Doris wiped her hands on her apron and hurried to answer it.

Outside, Gabe, a family friend, was standing on the step, smiling with a letter in hand. Gabe was a young man with bright eyes and an equally bright future ahead of him.

"Howdy, Mrs. Doris."

Doris grinned. No matter how old Gabe was, he was still that mischievous little boy in her Sunday School class.

"Hello, Gabe," Doris replied. "How are you? How are your folks?"

"They're swell, ma'am. How's Mr. Allen?"

"He's fine. He's tinkering away in the garage. Would you like to come inside? I just pulled out a tray of gingerbread and I could use an honest opinion of them."

"It's tempting, but I've got to get home. I just wanted to give this to you. Mike dropped this off our house by mistake."

Doris took the letter and beamed when she saw who it was from. "It's from Johnny! Thank you, Gabe!"

Gabe nodded and hesitated before asking, "When's the last you heard from Johnny?"

"Not since Thanksgiving." She held up the letter and smiled broadly. "But I'm hoping this is chock-full of news."

"So do I. I better be getting home. Merry Christmas, Mrs. Doris," he said as he started to leave. "Please say hi for me to Mr. Allen."

"Merry Christmas, Gabe. Send my love to your folks."

Doris closed the front door and anxiously tore into the letter. It was dated a couple of

129

weeks back. To her disappointment it was very short but it read:

Mom and Pop,

I'm doing great and staying plenty busy over here and I hope this finds you in good spirits. I want you to know that I'll be home for Christmas! I'm looking forward to your Christmas dinner, especially the pumpkin pie- with extra whip cream? I got to close now. Tell Pop I said hey and to be ready to lose at checkers! I love you both, Merry Christmas.

Your son,

Johnny Allen

Doris read it twice over and held it close to her heart. She was so overjoyed she felt as though she would burst.

"My Johnny's coming home," she whispered breathlessly.

Doris hurried to the garage to share the wonderful news. "Matthew! Matthew! Johnny's coming home for Christmas!"

Matthew looked up from the model airplane he was working on. "What's that now?" he asked with concern.

"A letter came from Johnny! He's going to be home for Christmas!" she cried happily as she thrust out the letter.

Matthew frowned as he read it. After a moment he handed it back to his wife.

"That's Johnny for you. We'll see just who loses at checkers this time." He chuckled as he went back to his work.

Though that was her husband's only reply, Doris knew without a shadow of a doubt that he was just as excited for their son's return.

Suddenly it dawned on her. "Christmas? That's tomorrow!" All at once a mental list of things that had to be done before his arrival took root in her mind and it grew at a rapid pace. "There's so much to do! I better get busy."

With that, she hurried back into her kitchen to finish what she'd started first.

Chapter 2

That evening Doris and Matthew sat together on the couch. In the corner, a short and squat tree was up and decorated with silver tinsel, a string of popcorn and a few store-bough ornaments. Pine needles littered the floor, as well as a number of strands of tinsel. Beneath the tree, there were three neatly wrapped packages.

A chipper fire danced in the fireplace, warming up the room and giving it a very homey feel. Although the radio was on, neither Doris nor Matthew paid it any mind. They were too preoccupied thinking of Johnny's return home and reminiscing past Christmas'

"You remember his very first Christmas?" Doris asked wistfully.

"He had no clue what was going on but he loved every minute of it."

Doris laughed, recalling a particular memory. "I was just thinking of the time when he knocked over the tree when he was trying to get to the angel on top."

Matthew nodded. "That look on his face when it fell down." He paused and added, "Do you remember the year he got that sling shot?"

Doris raised an eyebrow. "How could I forget? He broke my grandmother's table lamp."

"Our first checkers game," Matthew stated fondly.

Doris chuckled. "You should have seen the look on your face when you realized he had you beat."

"Yeah," Matthew answered with a content sigh.

There was a moment of silence as they savored the memories and anticipated the return of their son.

At that very moment, the doorbell rang. Doris and Matthew shot up from the couch. Doris opened the door and wept joyfully as she fell into her son's open arms.

The next hour was a blur of hugs, kisses, tears and warm welcomes. Doris tore herself away from Johnny's side to heat up some supper for him while father and son did some catching up.

Over a late supper of chicken fried steak and mashed potatoes, the family had a nice long talk and exchanged news, both local and foreign.

Even with all the talking, Johnny wolfed down his supper. "I haven't had a meal this good in months," he commented.

"Nothing beats your mother's cooking," Matthew bragged. Doris beamed. Not so much for the compliment, but it was just good having her boy home.

"How long can you stay?" she asked. "Gabe was asking after you. It would be nice if you two had the chance to catch up."

"I can't stay long at all. My unit ships back out in two days. I can only stay for Christmas day."

Doris was saddened by this news. After just getting her baby back, she wasn't ready to let him go that soon.

Matthew spoke up, breaking the silence. "Let's make the most of our time then. It's late. Why don't we all get a good night's sleep and we'll have all day tomorrow to enjoy?"

Johnny smiled and nodded in agreement. "It'll be great to sleep in my own bed again."

Christmas morning, the Allen family woke bright and early, eager to begin the day. While Doris whipped up a tasty breakfast of scrambled eggs, ham and toast, Johnny riffled through his duffle bag he'd brought home.

"When do you want to exchange presents?" he asked.

Doris briefly looked away from the skillet. "Now or later, makes me no difference to me. Ask your father."

Matthew looked up from yesterday's paper and shrugged. "Whenever you want to, son."

Johnny walked to the kitchen table, carrying two small items. "They're not wrapped, but I found these in an antique store in London…"

To Matthew, he gave a small metal tray shaped like a pop bottle cap. "It's not much, but you can put nails and screws in it while you're working in the garage."

To Doris, he handed her a silver spoon, elegantly decorated with pink roses. "To add to your spoon collection," Johnny explained.

Tearful hugs were exchanged while Matthew rose to get Johnny's gift from under the tree.

"This was supposed to be for your birthday in April, but after your mother read your letter, she went ahead and wrapped it up for you for now."

It was a care package, but not like the usual ones they often sent. This was filled with extras including paper, pens, playing cards, gum, and a few of sports magazines.

The day went by much too quickly. Johnny and Matthew played several games of checkers while the Christmas special was broadcasted over the radio. They spent the day playing cards, popping popcorn over the fire, and talking over old times.

After a filling Christmas dinner, and Johnny's much anticipated pumpkin pie with extra whip cream, it was time to call it a day.

It would be difficult saying goodbye to Johnny so soon, but Doris was thankful for the time they'd had together, no matter how brief.

Chapter 3

The next morning, Johnny was gone before morning. He'd taken his duffle bag and left without as much as a goodbye.

Doris cried over her untouched breakfast, missing her son terribly. Matthew was upset too, but for a different reason.

"It's not like Johnny to leave without saying goodbye. I wonder if something was wrong."

Troubled by this and with no way to contact her son, Doris cleared the table and busied herself with tiding up the kitchen. Matthew retreated to his garage to work on his project.

Not long after, the doorbell rang. Doris opened the door and saw a man in a crisp uniform. A telegram deliverer.

"Is this the home of Johnny Allen?" he asked stiffly.

Doris gave a look of confusion. "Yes?" The man handed over a yellow telegram, offered a short nod and left.

Doris closed the door and quietly read the telegram. Her heart caught in her throat and she screamed for Matthew.

Matthew came running into the living room. "What's wrong? What happened?" He saw the telegram in her hand.

Doris looked at him, tears misting in her eyes. "This has to be a mistake. Our Johnny was just here!"

Matthew took the telegram and read it for himself.

We regret to inform you that your son, Johnny Allen, was killed in a bombing in London.

Matthew studied it a while longer. "This happened just a few days ago."

"But Johnny was just home! How could he have been here when according to that…he was dead? It wasn't a dream, was it? He was here, wasn't he?"

Matthew nodded carefully. "Of course, he was here."

Doris returned to the kitchen. There was only one way to prove that Johnny had truly been there. She opened the cupboard where she kept her spoon collection. Doris scanned

139

the row, looking for the one Johnny had given her.

It wasn't there. Chills ran down her spine. It couldn't be possible.

She called out, "Matthew, where's the tray Johnny gave you?"

"On the shelf in the garage." Understanding the urgency in her tone, Matthew hurried to the garage. He returned empty-handed.

"Doris...you don't suppose that..." He couldn't even finish his thought.

"It's impossible! You don't think it's some sort of cruel prank, do you?"

Matthew automatically ruled this option out. "Johnny wouldn't do this. But..."

"But what?" Doris urged.

Matthew carefully framed his words. "Johnny did say he would be home for Christmas. Maybe this was his way of keeping his promise."

End

The Gallows

Left foot. Right foot. Left foot. Right foot.

I watch as my feet, black with dirt and grime from my cell, move slowly forward. How my feet keep moving is beyond me. The chains clink and clank with every miserable step.

My eyes flicker up for a brief moment. I can't pretend to ignore the screams and shouting that are directed at me. Insults fly left and right, hitting me like stones. A hanging is a special event and there's a large turnout for mine. No one wants to miss a cold-bloodied killer being brought to justice.

The problem is that I'm innocent...sort of. I did kill a man, but it was in self-defense. He was going to hurt my sister, Eliza. Governors' son or not, I had to save her.

I lift my head slightly and a sudden pain explodes in the back of my head. It's all I can do to keep silent. My vision blurs for a moment but clears up quickly.

"Keep yar head down, filth!"

I don't need to look behind me to see who my attacker is. It's my jailer, Theophilus. In his greasy hands, he keeps a large wooden club to deal out punishments or to just torment the prisoners. On inspection days, when the head jailer comes, Theophilus likes to use the spiked club with metal and glass shards, just for show. I can't even begin to recount how many times my back, arms and legs have been cut and slashed by that evil club.

Three years. I've been living in the bottom of a rat-infested, disease-ridden, prison. When I'm not being beaten and tortured, I'm shackled to the wall where the iron bites and tears at my raw skin. Moldy bread and dirty water are put out every day, but never within reach. The rats eat better than I do.

I focus on watching my feet again. The chains seem to grow heavier with every step. Theophilus jerks me to a stop by yanking on the end of my chain. I sneak a quick glance and see that I'm standing before the gallows.

The hatred around me only intensifies. The crowd is anxious to see me dead. They scream words like:

"Murderer!"

"Kill him!"

"String him up!"

I duck my head. They're only words, but I think they hurt worse than a beating. Why do people take such pleasure in violence? A sticky tear lands on my foot. I watch as it slides down, leaving a fresh white trail.

Theophilus pulls me forward and I take my first step up onto the wooden gallows.

"James! James!" a shrill voice screams among the crowd.

My heart sinks. I haven't seen Eliza since the trial, three years ago. As much as I miss her, I can't bear to see her.

"No, please! Don't kill him, he doesn't deserve this!" Eliza barges through the crowd until she's dead center and I have no choice but to face her. She's grown taller and more beautiful than the last time I saw her.

"Get lost, tramp!" Theophilus shouts at her.

My sister is no saint and I don't deny that she leads an impure life, but he has no right to call her that. A bubble of anger rises deep inside me.

Eliza pleads, "James! Tell them you were just defending me! Tell them!" Her cries are drenched in miserable tears.

Theophilus puts a rough and itchy thick rope around my neck and secures it. Can't Eliza see that there's no use in fighting? I'm a dead man.

"Any last words, filth?" Theophilus asks.

He wants me to beg for mercy or plead guilty, two things I've denied him the satisfaction of. Why give it to him now?

I look him in the eye and do something I've wanted to do since the first day he abused me. I spit directly in his eye. The surprise that washes over his face is priceless. His expression quickly darkens and without any warning he boxes me in the ear. I stagger back from the force and a splinter finds its way into my foot.

Eliza is sobbing uncontrollably. I wish she would go away. She isn't doing anyone any good.

A man I've never seen before stands next to me and reads aloud in a clear voice, my sentence.

I close my eyes, ready for the end. No matter what the judge says or what people believe, I know that I am innocent. I did nothing to deserve this death, but I will accept it because that is the destiny I have been dealt.

The floor beneath me instantly drops and I fall through. The rope around my neck stops me in mid fall, my feet dangling, and I feel my life fading away.

The last thing I see is my dear sister, Eliza. If only she knew how much more I wanted for her. She deserves better.

End

Bullied

Chapter 1

It was looking to be just another miserable day in school for Luke. Hiding in a bathroom stall during lunch, he silently nibbled at his food, grateful for a good lock on the door. Already that morning, he'd been tripped getting a seat on the bus, smacked in the back of the head in first period, shoved in a locker between classes, and twice his books were deliberately knocked out of his hands.

At least I didn't get beat up in the locker room like yesterday, he thought gloomily.

He swallowed a bite of his turkey sandwich, the bread sticking to the roof of his mouth. *How can I even say that? What gives them the right to bully me? I'm a human being too!* he silently declared.

The more he thought about it, the angrier he became. He hated his bullies. He hated the school. He hated himself for not fighting back. His hate reflected into the sandwich, as the soft white bread now had deep fingernail imprints.

His wrath subsided and despair took over. *Maybe they're right. Maybe I don't deserve to be happy.*

He suddenly threw his lunch on the green tile floor, disgusted with everything around him. Luke didn't care that his lunch slid outside the stall. He was too hurt and tired of it all to care. Folding his arms around his knees, he cried for the rest of lunch, not caring who heard him.

The bus ride home was always a horrible experience. As soon as he boarded, he took the first seat he could find nearest to the driver and curdled up in a ball beside the window, hoping that he would somehow be granted the gift of invisibility.

Most of the time this scheme worked and he went ignored because no bully in their right mind wanted to pick on a victim within earshot of the driver. But today, someone sat next to him.

Luke froze; his face to the window, hoping whoever it was would either go away or decide to be merciful.

Nothing happened. The engine of the bus roared to life and the scenery outside began to creep by.

He stole a timid glance and saw that his seat partner was a girl. She wasn't looking in his direction but from way she was cracking her knuckles and biting her bottom lip, she seemed anxious or upset about something. Luke turned away; ready to just ignore her when out of nowhere she started talking to him.

"Hi. My name's Lena." Her words came tumbling out as if she were uncertain about them.

Luke stared, dumbfounded. He couldn't remember the last time someone at school had said a kind word toward him.

"Umm…hi?" He noticed she was still cracking her knuckles and wondered if her strategy was to put him at ease first and then start beating him up.

Lena followed Luke's gaze and noticed she was cracking her knuckles. She stopped immediately. "It's a bad habit I picked up a while ago," she explained.

Luke shrugged. He wanted to blurt out, what do you want, just to get it over with, but that would be rude. Instead he leaned forward and rested his head on the back of the seat in front of him. This was the universal sign on the bus for, it's been a long day and I just want to be left alone.

Apparently, Lena was uneducated about this fact because she said, "I want to say I'm sorry. I watched when they shoved you in a locker. I felt awful and wanted to do something, but I just…couldn't. I'm sorry."

Luke sat up. No one had ever apologized to him before. "It's fine."

Lena firmly shook her head. "No, it's not fine. No one should be bullied and I'm sick of being a bystander."

Luke had no idea what to think. Was someone actually on his side? That would be a first.

"Have you ever told anyone?" Lena asked. "About being bullied?"

Luke shook his head. "What's the point? Nothing would change. It would probably make things worse."

"Not even your parents?" Lena replied in surprise.

"Have you ever been bullied?" Luke angrily interjected. "You wouldn't understand."

Lena was quiet for a moment before answering. "Actually, I do understand. At my old school I was constantly teased for my good grades. It got to the point where I began to fail just so the hateful words would stop. My parents found out when my teacher called about my failing grades and the truth came out when they confronted me. We moved here and things have been great ever since. Until I watched you getting bullied and I realized I was just as bad as them by not saying anything."

Luke mulled this over. He had, in fact, considered telling his parents. He'd played out several possible scenarios, all of them ending in a fiery explosion of doom. Even if things didn't end in doom, his pride always denied him of spilling his guts. To his mom and dad, he was popular at school and had tons of friends. He couldn't shed light on the reality that their only son was the school outcast. The shame would be too much.

"Were your parents mad at you when they found out?" he asked.

"They were only mad that I hadn't said anything in the first place and that I was letting the bullies win by failing on purpose."

The bus came to his stop much too quickly. As Luke stood, Lena moved aside to let him pass. She offered a sympathetic smile but said nothing.

Chapter 2

That evening the smell of greasy fried chicken warmed the house. Luke was starving and his stomach growled. His stomach was also in knots, but not from hunger.

Luke stared at his reflection in the bathroom mirror. A mental battle was raging in his mind. To tell his parents or to keep it to himself.

Maybe I shouldn't say anything, it will only make things worse. How many times had he heard this? A lot. The last thing he wanted was to give the bullies more reason to torment him. *Then again, what if that's just a myth and speaking up actually helps?* But there was still the shame he would feel admitting the truth. What if his parents laughed at him? Or were disappointed and said, it's your problem, you fix it.

There were too many things that could go wrong if he came out and told. *But if I keep it to myself, nothing will change.*

Every mean name he had been called since the bullying began came back to memory; the pain he felt when someone smacked, punched

154

or pinched him. Lastly, Lena's words rang out the loudest, *"No one should be bullied."* It was true and Luke knew it.

"Luke, dinner's ready!" his mom called from the kitchen.

He took a deep breath and backed away from the mirror. Luke was still considering what he would do when he entered the kitchen. His dad sat at the table, going over the mail while his mom was bringing a steaming plate of buttery rolls to the table.

Luke cleared his throat. Both his parents looked up. His mom gave him a warm smile, while his dad pulled out a chair beside him for him to come sit. The scene was proof of their love and it was enough to get the first words out.

"Mom, dad? I need to talk to you."

After dinner, Luke felt as if a heavy burden had been lifted from his weary shoulders. His dreaded secret was out and he no longer had to carry it alone.

But now the real question was… what now?

Both parents had listened carefully to their son's plight and were ready to give advice.

"You need to stand up for yourself. I'm not saying fight back, but show them that they can't mess with you," his dad said resolutely.

It sounded like a good idea, but how on earth would he do that?

His mom asked, "Do you know why some kids are bullies?"

Luke shrugged. "Because they're jerks?"

"No, honey. Because *they're* bullied and they want to take it out on someone else."

"Or they feel insecure and want to put someone down to make themselves feel better. Or they just want attention," Dad added.

This was news to Luke. "But the whole school can't feel that way. Everyone picks on me in some way or other."

"Everyone?" Mom asked skeptically.

Luke's mind automatically traveled back to the bus ride with Lena. "Well…. not *everyone*, but the majority of the school is against me."

"I bet its peer pressure," dad commented. "There's a ring leader, isn't there?"

Luke considered this. "You mean like the head bully? Caleb Dawes and his gang are the worst. He's popular so I guess everyone thinks it's cool to bully me if he does."

"Well, I'll tell you what we're going to do. Tomorrow, your father and I are taking you to school and we're going to talk to the principal and see what he suggests."

Luke's blood ran cold. "The principal? You're going all the way to the top?" Sure, it would save him a ride on the dreaded bus but this would surely cause a scene if the principal got involved.

Dad chuckled. "Not exactly the top, sport. But pretty close."

Mom stood up and started clearing away the dishes. "Get ready for bed, Luke. I know it's easier said than done, but don't stress about tomorrow. Get a good night's sleep."

Luke slowly stood up. How could he possibly sleep knowing what uncertainties tomorrow held?

"Luke?"

"Yeah, dad?"

"You did the right thing in coming to us about this. I know it wasn't easy but we're proud of you. Mom and I are both on your side. Don't forget that."

A small smile crept across Luke's face. He needed to hear this. It made a world of difference. "Thanks dad. Thanks mom. Love you guys."

Chapter 3

In Luke's entire career as a student, he'd never set foot in the principal's office. He felt like he was in trouble and had to keep reminding himself that he wasn't.

It was just after five-thirty in the morning and the school was empty except for teachers and staff who were arriving in small clusters or one by one. Not even the buses were lined up in the semi-circle shaped driveway yet.

Luke and his parents were sitting in Mr. Perkins' office, having been told by the secretary that he'd stepped out momentarily but would be with them right away.

Mr. Perkins' office didn't look scary. It looked like a regular office with a desk, swivel chair, filing cabinets, and a lot of Woodard Middle School spirit decorating the walls: pennant flags, framed newspaper clippings announcing wins and achievements, and several pictures of different teams and clubs, not just sports and the popular clubs but some Luke hadn't even heard of, like the chess team.

The chess team, according to the picture, consisted of three boys who would be socially defined as nerds.

While Luke was wondering where and when the chess team met, the door opened and Mr. Perkins walked in.

"Sorry to keep you all waiting." He shook hands with each of them, including Luke, and sat down behind his desk. "What can I do for you all?"

Luke's mom got straight to the point and carefully explained everything. Luke watched the principal's expression, expecting to see amusement, annoyance, or outright disbelief. But all he saw was a thoughtful expression of one who was listening carefully to every word.

When mom was finished, Mr. Perkins looked directly at Luke. "I'm sorry you're going through this. I want you to know I'm going to do everything in my power to put a stop to this. I don't tolerate bullying in my school."

For the next fifteen minutes or so, the four of them discussed possible solutions. All of them agreed that running from the problem wasn't the answer. Facing it head-on was the best strategy.

"If a bully knows they have the upper hand, they'll keep it up. But once they realize they've lost their hold over you; odds are that they will stop," Mr. Perkins explained. "Believe it or not, I was a target in middle school too. I know how ruthless kids can be."

He picked up something on his desk that had been hidden from view and placed it in front. "This quote, among others, helped me through a lot of tough times. It might help you too."

Luke read the wooden plaque aloud. "Courage is not the absence of fear but the acquired ability to move beyond fear."

"Do you know what that means?" the principal asked gently.

Luke shook his head.

"It means that it's *okay* to have courage and still be afraid. Fear is good in some aspects. It keeps us alert and cautious but if we let it control our lives, we become a slave to it. Courage is facing that fear and saying, you have no power over me anymore. Do you understand?"

"I think so."

Mr. Perkins nodded. "I'm going to make an announcement during homeroom, addressing the seriousness of bullying. If this persists, don't hesitate to come to me."

Handshakes went around once more and after leaving the office and saying quick goodbyes to his parents, Luke headed to his locker to get his books for homeroom. The halls were still empty and it was strange to be able to walk to class without having to be on constant alert.

Is this how other kids feel all the time? Carefree and at ease? Must be nice.

Chapter 4

As promised, a blaring announcement went out through the intercom during homeroom. Mr. Perkins didn't name names, but he did remind the school that bullying was wrong and that there were severe consequences.

Luke tried to act causal. As though he were just as surprised as his classmates to hear this random announcement, but he felt their stares and heard their whispering. He wasn't fooling anyone. They knew.

The school day inched by and Luke was on pins and needles, preparing for the worst. So far no one had said a single word to him or got near him.

It wasn't until the last class that he allowed himself to let down his guard. Was it really going to be this easy? Luke decided he could live out the rest of his school days invisible. He'd have Lena to talk to on the bus and that would be enough.

The final bell rang and school was officially over. He took a deep breath and allowed a smile. *I guess all that worrying was for nothing.*

He followed the steady stream of kids outside and soaked in the warm sunshine. It was a good day.

"Hey, Luke!" Caleb Dawes called out.

Just like that, the storm clouds rolled in and his whole body tensed up. Caleb, the ringleader, was leaning against the corner of the building.

Caleb waved him over, his tone dripping with malice. "Come here, buddy. I want to talk to you."

Inside, a voice was screaming for him to run to the bus. He would be safe on the bus. But would he really ever be safe? He couldn't avoid Caleb forever. Unless one of them moved away, they would be in the same school, same grade level until graduation. And then what? Bullies just didn't live in schools. They were everywhere: college, the grocery store, at work…eventually he would encounter one. But if he could stand up to this one, maybe the next one would be easier.

Much against his good judgment, he walked towards Caleb. Mr. Perkin's quote flashed in his mind. *Courage is not the absence of fear but the acquired ability to move beyond fear.*

Luke was well aware he was walking into a trap, but he had no idea just how *big* a trap it was. Around the corner, an angry mob was in position, ready to nab him and beat him to a pulp.

Before he knew it, Luke was surrounded, pushed around until his back was to the wall. They were shouting at him, calling him names and threatening him. The voices blended as one and Luke couldn't distinguish one from the other. They were like sharks, just itching for the first scent of blood so they could attack.

Fear didn't begin to describe what Luke was feeling. Terror was more like it. Terror and regret. Luke regretted telling his parents and the principal. This is what happened when you spoke up.

Caleb was the solo authority; that much was obvious. He entered the circle and the shouting died down. Everyone looked to him, waiting for further instructions. If he'd told them all to get on the ground and act like dogs, they would have obeyed without giving it a second thought. The control he had over them was disgusting.

The control he has over me is disgusting too. What was it that Mr. Perkins said about control? Luke couldn't remember but he knew the gist of it.

Caleb threw several punches, the mob cheering him on. Luke tried to block his face but failed miserably. His face throbbed with pain and he felt blood starting to trickle from his nose. The back of his head didn't feel too good either from hitting against the brick wall.

Caleb took a step back. "You think you can rat me out and get away with it just like that?"

Luke wiped at his nose, smearing the blood. In all the abuse, this was the first time they drew blood. This was the final straw.

Trembling as he was, Luke managed to say, "I'm not going to let you or anyone else bully me anymore."

Caleb burst out laughing. This encouraged the others to laugh as well until Caleb didn't find it funny anymore.

"Aww, did your mommy and daddy tell you to say that?"

Luke took an intimidating step towards Caleb, who, in turn, took an involuntarily step back. "I'm not afraid of you anymore." Luke scanned the silent crowd and added. "And you all shouldn't be afraid of him either."

Luke's bravery was rewarded with the first glimpse of confusion and uneasiness. Encouraged by the response, he continued. "Why do you let him control you? Because he thinks he's popular? Because he thinks he's cool? He's not any better than you and I." As he talked, he kept walking towards Caleb, who was hastily backing away. Caleb's confidence was long gone and fear shown in his eyes.

Caleb stopped abruptly when he backed into the side of the dumpster. Frantically, he looked around for support from his followers but they were just as stunned.

On an impulse Luke brought up a tight fist and Caleb immediately screamed for mercy and shielded his face. This was a side of Caleb no one had ever seen. Luke remembered what his mom had told him, about bullies being bullied themselves.

167

Luke lowered his fist. "I'm not going to hit you. I'm not a bully."

Caleb slowly lowered his hands from his revealing a snot and tear-stricken face. Here, the big and bad bully was brought down to tears by his own victim. Luke knew all too well what shame and humiliation felt like.

He faced the crowd and motioned for them to leave. "Go away. There's nothing to see."

In actuality, there was plenty to see but they reluctantly obeyed but not before giving Caleb strange looks. A few laughed at him.

Once they were alone, Luke turned back to Caleb, who was busy trying to wipe away all signs of his moment of weakness.

Point-blank, Luke asked, "Why?"

Caleb spit on the ground. "Why what, twerp?"

"Why do you think it's alright to bully someone else just because you get bullied at home?"

Caleb's expression darkened. "What do you know about my life? Nothing!"

"I know enough to recognize fear when I see it," he quietly answered. "The way you covered your face and screamed like I was going to kill you- you've done that before. At home?"

Neither boy said anything.

Finally, Caleb relaxed and said, "You're lucky, Luke."

"Me? I've been bullied every day since the beginning of the school year. How's that lucky?"

"You've got a cheering section."

Luke frowned. "I don't get it."

"Last year at field day, you struggled just to keep up in every race. It was pathetic. But at the awards, when you got nothing but a lousy participation ribbon, your parents ate it up like you were some kind of super athlete."

"But you placed first in almost every event," Luke pointed out.

Caleb glared at Luke. "I fought to win just to prove to my dad that I was a winner and what did he do? He told me I was a worthless loser. He crumbled up my awards and threw them back in my face."

169

Caleb sneered hatefully. "I bet your folks even took you out for ice cream to celebrate."

Luke was at a loss for words. They had gone out for ice cream and his dad had told him, win or lose, as long as you do your best, we're proud of you, sport.

Caleb wiped at his eyes. "So, you're lucky. You get to go home to a nice family. You can talk to your parents. I don't have anyone..."

"You have Mr. Perkins," Luke blurted.

"The principal?" Caleb asked incredulously. "Yeah right!"

"No, really," Luke insisted. "He's a good guy."

Caleb shook his head. "That kind of thing might work for people like you, but not for me."

Chapter 5

After a mad dash, Luke just barely made it to his bus. He didn't have to tell Lena what happened. The news had spread like wildfire, but with several varying stories, all highly exaggerated.

At home, he told his parents everything, holding nothing back. As badly as Luke wanted to help Caleb, both mom and dad explained that this was a different kettle of fish and it would have to be handled delicately.

When Luke suggested talking to Mr. Perkins *for* Caleb, they put an immediate kibosh on that plan.

"No one can do that for him," Mom explained. "He has to want to speak up, just like you did. No one could have gone in your place. But you can be there to listen to his problems and encourage him to get help. That in itself will go a long way."

This advice turned out to be the best they could have offered. After a few weeks, Caleb came to trust and depend on Luke.

Not long after, Caleb decided that enough was enough and he asked Luke to go with him to see Mr. Perkins. It was the meeting that would change Caleb's life for the better. He had to cross some rough storms, but in the end, he said that his only regret was not befriending Luke sooner.

Caleb's situation went on to impact Luke as well. With a personal passion for justice, and a lot of support from his family and friends, he worked his way through college, graduated with honors, and became the guidance consular at Woodard Middle School.

On his desk in his office, placed for all to see, he kept a wooden plaque, a gift from a dear friend. It read:

Courage is not the absence of fear but the acquired ability to move beyond fear.

End

The Rebel

Chapter 1

"Get away from that window!"

My mom's frightful command startles me and I back away, letting the black plastic covering fall back into place.

"I just wanted to see why the tank was stopping," I reason.

Mom is too busy with dinner now to answer. Or maybe she just isn't in the mood to talk about tanks.

It's not a strange sight to see military tanks patrolling up and down the road. But if the tank slows or comes to a stop, depending on the time of day, it means that someone is either breaking curfew or performing illegal activities, such as playing toss in the yard or tending to a flower garden. Technically it's not against the law to have a tiny flower garden; vegetable gardens are prohibited because of the risk of radiation in the ground. Officials would have to come out to check the soil and that's too much of a hassle.

The rule of thumb when it comes to gardening is to not get caught. I just hope whoever decided to risk their life was wearing their microwatch.

Grandpa, sitting in his recliner, comes to my defense as usual. "It ain't no sin to look out your own window, Becky. I remember when you could have up curtains and window clings. Heck, there was even a time when you could open the blasted things."

"What are window clings, Grandpa?" I've heard about curtains. They sound much nicer than our coverings we have to have now.

"They're like stickers for your window. They had 'em for all seasons and holidays. And sun catchers! I forgot about snatchers."

I'm about to ask what a sun catcher is but mom tells us to stop rehashing the past and it's time to eat.

I know I'm luckier than most kids because I have a grandparent who remembers what he calls the glory days. He likes to tell me about things like parades, picnics, and theaters. About a time when dozens of complete strangers could gather in one building, without the required safe suit, order how much, or how little, food they wanted from a large selection and sit within spitting distance without any barriers or protective shields around them. But that's what Grandpa calls a restaurant.

Sometimes I think he makes up a lot of it because it's pretty hard to imagine. Still, it'd be nice to pick and choose what I want to eat. This week our assigned dinner ingredients are canned pork with a pasty gravy, canned bread and canned artificial green beans.

The food rations are delivered every Sunday, direct from the government. I sure hope next week we get some beef. That's my favorite. Grandpa insists that this isn't real food. I personally haven't had any other kind so I wouldn't know. It tastes real enough to me.

Mom looks up from her plate and stares at Grandpa. "I know it's not a sin to look out a window, dad. But there are some things an eleven-year-old doesn't need to see."

I want to ask what these mysterious things are but I don't. Not in front of mom. Maybe I can get Grandpa to tell me later. He doesn't treat me like a kid, but like another human being. He says he doesn't want me to grow up believing that this is the best that life has to offer.

176

Grandpa has to be pretty lonely. I think he's the one his age still alive. People don't live very long. Once you reach fifty, you're basically a walking time bomb, ready to go off at any moment. Mom's thirty-seven. Grandpa's seventy-two.

During his early years, life was what he called "normal" but shortly after mom was born, things started to happen. Constant famines, diseases, and radiation. The world was going to end.

Until Madam Olivia Silis came into power in 2035, fifteen years ago, and started making things better and safer. It probably won't happen in my lifetime, but one day everything is going to change for the better. At least that's what my virtual educator says. They also say that no place is safe as long as we continue to exist. Hearing this always makes me uncomfortable. I want to live in safety, but how can I enjoy it if I don't exist?

I've asked Grandpa was he thinks it means and he just tells me to ignore the socialist propaganda and stay under the radar, whatever that means.

Dinner is good. Not because of the food, which tastes like it always does, but because there's no debating or arguments.

Grandpa likes to go off on a tangent, as mom calls it. He complains about everything from the safe suits to the Tive, which is a spray that must be applied once a day to protect us from radiation. Twice a day depending on your current medical condition.

Grandpa's always saying that our rights have been stolen right from under us and no one so much as raised an eyebrow. He's an angry and bitter minority because no one really knows what he's talking about because he's older.

Who knows? Maybe there are other older people out there and we just don't know it because outdoor communication is basically nonexistent and virtual communication is pretty strict too. Unless it's for school or work, and even then, no one shares pictures or uses their real name. We sign in using our number which was assigned with our all-in-one-vaccine. I'm number 8365210947, but I prefer to go by Megan.

After a quiet dinner it's time to gather around the T.V and wait for the news. There's only one source of news, in order to protect us from biased lies and treachery, and it's broadcasted every night from six-thirty to seven and at seven oh five- it's lights out.

"Don't forget to record your dinner, Megan," mom reminds. As if I need reminding.

I look down at the microwatch on my wrist- a black and bulky hunk of lightweight, environmentally-friendly, plastic. It only takes a moment to put in that I ate dinner.

The microwatch is an everyday essential tool. There's a location tracker in case you get lost or kidnapped, a food counter to keep your weight in check and a spray alarm that goes off nonstop everyone morning until you either hit remind me later or just get up and get it over with. My favorite feature is a game called Lucky Leaper. Grandpa says it's just a cheap knock off on an old game called Frogger. Either way, it's still fun.

We settle in and the news comes on. Grandpa says there used to be actual people on T.V called reporters and news anchors who would give the news. As I watch the big bold words slowly scroll up the screen, I try to imagine this but it's hard. Not to mention how awkward it would be to report the news in a safe suit.

A safe suit is a big yellow plastic suit with lots of padding. There's a full-face glass helmet and an oxygen tank strapped to the back in case the air gets a bit thin inside the helmet. Safe suits are expensive, hard to find, and a strict requirement if you intend on taking more than five steps out your door. You can't try to make your own either. Each one has to come from a factory where they are certified. It may seem like a hassle, but it's all for our protection. The air quality outside is bad, the ozone is letting off poisonous gases and the ground is riddled with radiation. It too dangerous to stay outside for long without one.

The news consists of the usual updates: Reminders to spray Tive, followed by an advertisement for a special lotion to help with the dry and irritated skin caused by Tive. This is followed by the current count of radiation deaths today, three thousand and two- which makes a total of almost five billion. Here's something interesting, the arrest of a radical citizen who went out for a walk in his neighborhood with the excuse of wanting to get some fresh air.

A few other reminders and recommendations are shown before it clicks off. Like clockwork we move to go to our bedrooms, when suddenly the T.V comes to life again. We exchange confused looks and stay glued to our seats, waiting for something to happen. It doesn't take long.

I've only seen a picture Madam Silis but she has a face that you won't forget; from her flaming red hair to the shockingly stern and sharp features. Madam Silis is on the screen now, not quite frowning, but certainly upset.

"Citizens, it grieves me deeply to know that there are some radical-minded individuals who are attempting to spread false, inaccurate and harmful information to the general public via an unauthorized form of newsprint they call, Freedom News.

"These selfish and dangerous radicals are a threat to our society. If you have been approached or asked to take a copy, you are required by law to report them to your county officials. In the meantime, to root out this problem, in-home searches will begin tomorrow. Officials will be searching for the following: illegal newsprint propaganda, Any and all tools or equipment capable of creating said propaganda, and any unauthorized weapons. Thank you and goodnight."

I'm the only one who doesn't know what's going on. Mom looks scared. Grandpa is pale and looks like he's going to be sick.

"What did she mean?" I ask.

My question goes unanswered. Instead mom turns on Grandpa.

"I told you there'd be trouble if you kept printing those. Didn't I say, Dad, you need to quit while you're ahead?" Her voice is trembling and she's close to tears.

I wait for Grandpa to give her a snappy comeback but he doesn't. He stands up and heads to the front door.

"You can't go outside after lights out!" I shout. My Grandpa might be a rebel in his own way but this is just reckless.

I have no idea what's going on or where Grandpa is going, but mom must know because she jumps to her feet and stands in front of the door, blocking his way.

"Don't you see? This is how they're trying to weed you out. If you go out now the

patrols will shoot you on sight. Wait until
daylight. Please."

I glance at the T.V and back at Grandpa,
the wheels in my head spinning. He's not one
of those radicals Madam Silis was talking
about, is he? I know he gets angry but he's
not selfish or dangerous. You have a right to
be angry, don't you?

Suddenly, there's a loud bang outside and
a woman is screaming. You don't hear
gunfire very often, but it's unmistakable.

"Mom?" My voice is barely above a
whisper.

Mom's sobbing now. Grandpa holds her
close and promises he won't do anything
foolish. This seems to alleviate her fears and
we get ready for bed.

I lay awake in the dark, listening to moms
sniffling; Grandpa's tossing and turning in the
next room, and the powerful tanks slowly
cruising the road. Blinding search lights beam
through the window- cutting through the
black plastic- and light up the room before
moving away.

For the first night that I can remember, I
go to bed feeling afraid.

Chapter 2

It's morning when I wake up and last night feels like just a horrible nightmare. We go about our day as normal. We spray our Tive, record breakfast on our microwatches, and I turn on my tablet, ready for another day of school.

Mom's at work in her room. The door is closed, a sign that she's in a virtual conference meeting and is not to be disturbed for anything. Grandpa's in the restroom, I think.

It doesn't take long to sign in and join the lecture. My virtual educator reminds us that today is national authority appreciation day and that we should take the time to appreciate those in authority over us because they are selflessly sacrificing their time and lives for us and for those ungrateful radicals. I know my virtual educator is referring to the ones Madam Silis spoke of.

One of the students, number 5398760124, buzz in with a statement and the virtual educator allows them to type. Words appear across the top of the screen.

The radicals are trying to destroy our way of life. They must be stopped at all costs.

My virtual educator types back, *you are correct, 5398760124. Class, how can we, as mere children, do our part to put a stop to these radicals? This question is worth fifteen percent of your grade.*

Suggestions fly across the screen. *Turn them in. Destroy their newspaper. Report them. Kill them.*

I suddenly feel very ill. My number pops up and the virtual educator says that I haven't contributed yet. How would I stop a radical?

Carefully, I type the words: *I could just ignore them.*

But, 8365210947, that won't stop them from persuading the weak and helpless among us. They must be stopped for the greater good.

But what's wrong with just ignoring them and letting them be angry. They're allowed to be angry and have an opinion.

Before I can send this through, Grandpa jumps in and deletes my response. "What did

I tell you about staying under the radar, Megan?"

"I'm only repeating things you've said," I explain defensively. I thought he would be proud to hear I was 'fighting the system' as he calls it.

"You just tell them what they want to hear, understand? Go on, tell them they're right and you're wrong."

"But, grandpa…" I've never seen him like this. What's the word? Compliant?

"Either you do it or I will," he says angrily.

Confused and stunned by this order, I type, *you're right. The radicals must be stopped.*

My virtual educator replies, *yes, 8365210947. How will you do your part to stomp them out?*

Grandpa is still by my side. "Tell 'em you'll find out where they live, put on your safe suit, and burn down their house with them, their family and all their evil lies inside."

I whirl around in my seat. "Grandpa! How can I say something like that?"

"Trust me. They'll eat it up and they won't think twice about questioning where you stand."

Hesitantly I type the harsh words. It doesn't take long for the comments of approval to come in.

Perfectly savage, 8365210947. A plus for ingenuity.

Grandpa pats my back. "What'd I tell you?" he says grimly. "These lunatics crave violence."

"But that was horrible. And you always say that we *do* have opinions. You didn't make that up, did you?" I can't imagine him lying about that.

Despite his bad knee, grandpa kneels down at my level and takes my hand in his. "Listen to me, Megan. I've never once lied to you. But it's very dangerous to say things like that. Especially right now. More than ever, we need to watch what we say."

"Grandpa, tell me the truth. Are you one of those radicals on the news? Are you in danger?"

"I'm not in any more danger now, than when I served in World War 3. Now you just focus on your learning and don't worry about me."

Instead of reassuring me, his answer only scares me. But I tell him otherwise. Grandpa struggles to his feet and takes a seat in his recliner. He takes a nap and I go back to my schooling.

Mom's meeting ends just before dinner, which always makes her irritable because she has to hurry and flusters easily. If there's anything mom hates, it's being flustered.

"Megan, wake Grandpa up and tell him dinner's almost ready."

Grandpa's still in his recliner. I guess kneeling on the floor really wore him out. I gently shake his shoulder.

"Grandpa? Mom says it's time to wake up."

Suddenly our front door flies open and a team of five people, donned in the necessary equipment, barge in and spread out around the house. Mom screams. Grandpa's eyes flash open and he's on his feet in seconds. All I can think is that I've never seen so many people in one place before. Is this sort of what it must have felt like to be in a restaurant? Minus the fear and uncertainty.

Mom runs to our side and holds me close. She's muttering something between her sobs. Is she praying? Mom's never prayed before. We stand together while the men do a full search of our home.

The search consists of knocking over chairs, breaking dishes, shattering picture frames and ripping apart sheets and pillows. The chaos is frightening. Mom's tears land on my arm and I feel grandpa's rough old callused hand tighten on shoulder. He shouts at them to stop, but it does no good.

One of the inspectors approaches us and order us to leave the house. When we don't move as quickly as expected, we're roughly shoved out. More inspectors are waiting outside and we're immediately handcuffed and placed in separate cars. My emotions are out of control. Not only am I a long way outside and in a car, two things I've never done before, but I'm in huge trouble.

From my window I watch as my home begins to burn. The five inspectors exit safely, a blazing inferno growing behind them. In the blink of an eye, everything I've ever known is gone. All I can really focus on is the lie I told to my virtual educator this morning.

I would find out where they live, put on my safe suit, and burn down their house with them, their family and all their evil lies inside.

Guilt eats at me quicker than the greediest fire can consume. *Is this all my fault?*

Chapter 3

We've been taken to a facility somewhere far away and told to wait. We're no longer handcuffed, but I think that's because we're being watched by two heavily armed guards who look like the type who could pull a puppy's tail and laugh when it whimpers. I can't help but think it's strange that neither of these guards is wearing a safe suit or a microwatch.

I want to ask Grandpa a million and one questions but I don't dare with the guards around. Is this what Grandpa meant by being careful what we say?

I keep my mouth closed and wait for this nightmare to end. Mom's still sobbing. I rub her back to comfort her, the way she's done for me, but it doesn't work. I guess some tears are stronger than others.

Suddenly, the three of us are called into separate rooms. A pretty young woman is waiting for me. She smiles brightly and urges me to have a seat at the table. Despite her inviting smile, it's easy to see the malice behind it. She also isn't wearing a safe suit, but there is a microwatch on her wrist.

"Do you prefer to go by your birth name or your assigned number?"

I start to answer the obvious but Grandpa's words call out in my mind like a warning bell, *you just tell them what they want to hear, understand? Go on, tell them they're right and you're wrong.*

I confidently answer, "My number, of course."

She nods and taps something on the screen of her tablet. I can't tell if she's pleased or disappointed in my answer.

"Alright, 8365210947. I'm number 9105784326. I'm going to ask you a series of questions. Just be honest and we'll be finished quickly."

"First, how are you? Do you feel sick? What are your current emotions right now?"

I timidly raise my hand. "Actually, before we start can you please tell me why my family and I are here?"

"You're here to answer these questions, silly!" She calls me silly as if I'm a senseless child who doesn't know how to put on a microwatch. If that's the way she sees me, then that's what she's going to get.

She continues. "Let's talk about you, 8365210947. Do you like school?"

I shrug. "It's alright."

"What do you do for fun? Do you have any hobbies?"

"What's a hobby?"

"A hobby is something enjoyable you do. Like drawing, or reading, or writing…"

"I like sleeping. And eating," I say thoughtfully. "Do those count as hobbies?"

Her smile flickers but she nods cheerfully and records that on her tablet. "Do you love your country and those in power?"

"Today is national authority appreciation day," I say with a sheepish grin.

"It certainly is, 8365210947. Tell me, have you ever owned, purchased, borrowed, shared, or aided in any way in the making of Freedom News?"

"Freedom News? What's that?"

"Madam Silis spoke of this the other night. You must have heard about it."

"Oh, that. No."

"No what?" She looks at me as if I'm nuts.

"No, I've never owned, purchased, borrowed, shared, or aided in any way in the making of Freedom News." I add, "What's it about anyway?"

Her smile is replaced with an icy stare. "Lies and rubbish."

I can't resist asking, with as much innocence as I can muster, "Oh, have you read a copy of it?"

"Next question." Her sweet and charming tone is completely gone now. "What does your mother do?"

"She cleans the house, cooks the meals…"

"For a *living*."

"Oh. She works at a virtual retail store. She does a bit of everything from being a virtual greeter to cleaning out the virtual fitting rooms."

The woman types all this in. "Has your mother ever used words such as: tyranny, dictatorship, freedom, rebellion, rights, constitution, opinion, or religion? If so, provide an example of how it was used."

I pretend to think this over carefully before answering, "Nope."

"What about your grandfather?"

I frown curiously. "What about him?"

She sets her tablet on the table hard and gives me a dirty look. "Young lady, if you are purposely attempting to avoid answering my questions, then I will have no choice but to mark you down for uncooperativeness. Do you understand the seriousness of that?"

She opens her mouth, I assume it's to further explain the seriousness involved, but just then there's a frantic knock on the door and a middle-aged man throws open the door. He looks from me to my interrogator and back again.

"What is it, 57193620458? I'm in the middle of something very important."

His mouth opens and closes like he's gasping for breath. "It's Madam Silis. She's…she's…been assassinated!"

Chapter 4

I wasn't supposed to hear that. One look at the woman's face is enough to tell me that. Our questions come to an abrupt end and I'm ordered to wait in the room.

Assassinated? Isn't that a complicated word for murdered? Killed? If so, who did it and how and why? Conflicting thoughts run through my mind. Didn't all of my virtual class want to kill the radicals because they didn't agree with them? Just because you don't agree with someone, does it give you the right to kill that person?

I'm in the middle of sorting these thoughts out, when the T.V screen in the back of the room flickers to life. A real-life person is on the T.V. Just like grandpa said used to happen.

He isn't wearing a safe suit or a microwatch.

"Madam Silis has not been assassinated, as is being claimed. She passed away minutes ago due to spraying Tive into a cut. The poisonous chemical entered her bloodstream, instantly shutting down her system.

"Patriots, I'm calling to you to answer the call for freedom. We've been under the thumb of tyrants for far too long. Will you take back your country, in this, their moment of weakness? As we speak, the Silis Mansion and the One World Center are being surrounded, and these criminals are being arrested. Join us in person or tune in for hourly updates."

The T.V turns off and all I can do is stare at the blank screen, trying to figure out what it all means.

Just then, the door opens again and this time Grandpa bursts in. Mom's standing in the doorway, smiling and dabbing at her eyes.

"Did you hear that, Megan? We won!" He wraps me up in a tight, bone-crushing hug.

"But Grandpa, what's it all mean for us? What did we win?" I ask as soon as I can breathe again.

He sits down beside me and pats my arm. I can't remember the last time he looked so happy.

"It means we're going to be free again. It means you've got a very bright future ahead of you."

"So…" I consider my question a moment before asking. "So, does that mean I can eat inside a restaurant someday?"

Grandpa laughs, loud and carefree. "The second that one starts up again, I'll take you and your mom and you can order anything you want."

End

Love Letters in the Attic

Chapter 1

The attic ladder squeaked under foot as Kim and her husband, Brandon, made several trips back and forth, bringing down boxes, crates, old furniture and a large streamer trunk and setting them all in the garage.

After seven happy years in the historical home, Kim and Brandon decided it was time to move and the last thing that needed to be done was to clean out the dusty attic.

While the house was beautiful and spacious, it was also, unfortunately, becoming a deathtrap. Built in the early nineteen-hundreds, it still had old gas lines and oil lamps attached to the walls in the hall. Mold grew in the cellar; small amounts of asbestos were in the wallpaper in the sitting room and most recently, one of the steps on the staircase gave way beneath Kim. The house was in sore need of repairs and a modern renovation. It was cheaper to move than to restore the house.

Brandon set a wooden crate on top of a stack of other crates and dusted off his hands. "Looks like this is the last of it."

Kim was studying the steamer trunk she'd instantly fell in love with. Even though it was old and the hinges were rusty, it was beautiful with its vine design. Kim wondered who it belonged to and where they'd traveled to with it. Paris? Germany? Australia?

She looked up at Brandon and nodded. "And a good thing too. Now we just have to go through everything."

The house had several owners over the years and apparently not one of them had ever thought to clean out the attic, but they didn't have a problem adding to the clutter.

There was no telling what sort of historical treasures there might be. Anything of interest or value would be sold to an antique shop or go to auction.

"How about we grab some lunch before we start digging through all this?" Brandon suggested.

"Sounds like a plan. Let me grab a shower first."

After a quick lunch of greasy burgers and floppy fries, Kim and Brandon were ready to begin.

It took longer than it should have because Kim liked to pick up every item, examine it and wonder who'd had it last and what happened to them and things like that. There were a lot of papers, clothes, tools, bedrails, toys and contraptions. It was obvious that a vast span of generations had added to the attic over time. From an old gramophone to a box of presidential campaign buttons from the fifties.

Inside a cardboard box filled with collectable model cars, Kim discovered a pile of unopened envelopes all tied together in twine. On top of the stack, was a single dried rose.

Kim was instantly intrigued over the find. All of them were addressed to a Dorothy Kingsley at the current address.

"Brandon, look at these," she exclaimed as she handed them to him. "Whoever Dorothy was, she never opened them."

Brandon was less than enthusiastic. Unlike Kim, he wasn't interested in any of the previous owners or their belongings. He just wanted to finish the job so they could move.

He shrugged and handed them back. "I doubt there's much value in those. You can toss them."

"Toss them? These could be very valuable. Perhaps not in terms of monetary, but in sentiment. Just look at the rose. I bet these are love letters! Forgotten love letters that were either never sent. Or poor Dorothy never had the chance to open them."

Brandon sighed. "Whatever the story behind them, they're useless to us now. Unless you want to open them for yourself…"

Kim was outraged by such a suggestion. "I can't read someone's love letters! That's as bad as reading someone's diary."

Kim looked over them once more. "I don't see a date on these, but they're all from a Mr. Thomas Young."

"That's nice, dear." Brandon had already moved onto a collection of vinyl records and was flipping through them.

Kim was playing around with an idea. "I wonder…wouldn't it be something to hand deliver these to Dorothy? If she's still alive, I mean."

"Look, Kim. We've got enough to do already without adding the task of finding some random old lady and playing matchmaker. Besides, she's probably passed away a long time ago. Those letters look pretty old."

Kim knew there was no sense in arguing. As much as she loved Brandon, he lacked imagination. She held onto the letters, determined to do a bit of research and see if she could locate Dorothy Kingsley.

Chapter 2

With a bit of determination and hard work, Kim was able to track down a list of the previous owners. The house was built in eighteen-ninety-nine and since then it had passed from six different owners. As much as Kim would have liked to dwell on all the owners, she had to focus on one in particular: Mr. and Mrs. William Kingsley and their only child, Dorothy. They lived in the house from nineteen twenty-six till fifty-eight. A total of thirty-two years.

Being a reporter, Kim loved doing research and with each new bit of information, it became easier and easier to track Dorothy down.

According to her research, Dorothy had married a well-to do young man, name of McCarthy, at the tender age of seventeen in nineteen forty-two. They lived together until McCarthy's death in ninety-four.

As far as Kim knew, Dorothy was still alive and was a current resident at Mossy Oaks Nursing Home. In four months, she was due to celebrate her ninety-fifth birthday.

Kim didn't bother keeping Brandon in the loop with each new gold nugget of information. He wouldn't have cared anyway.

The next logical step was to call and see if it was alright to visit Dorothy. The nursing home wasn't far, two hours' drive at the most.

Before she called, Kim stopped to wonder if this was a wise decision. Dorothy was nearing one-hundred years old. What if whatever those letters contained only brought her sorrow? Did she really need to be reminded of a painful past? On the other hand, this could bring the lady news she's been waiting to hear all these years.

In the end Kim decided that after all her hard work; it would criminal not to see this through. Besides, if she were Dorothy, she'd want the letters, no matter what they might contain.

Chapter 3

Two days later, Kim was sitting in the waiting area of Mossy Oaks Nursing home, waiting to be taken back to Dorothy's room. Kim kept the letters in her purse and resisted the temptation to pull them out and study them for the hundredth time.

Thankfully, she didn't have to wait long. The nurse, who went to notify Dorothy of her visitor, beckoned Kim to follow.

"It is unusual for Dorothy to have visitors," the nurse commented as they walked down the hall.

"Doesn't she have any remaining family members?" Kim asked.

"None that are on file, besides her great-niece who brought her here. But that was almost seven years ago and she hasn't been back since." The nurse seemed annoyed by this fact.

The nurse went on to say, "I'm glad you're here though. It'll do her good to have a visitor."

The two women stopped in front of a plain wooden door. The nurse knocked, and then slowly opened the door.

"Miss. Kingsley, your visitor, Kim Lawson, is here."

Kim automatically noticed the little thin figure sitting in the white wicker chair beside the window. Her back was to them. The nurse smiled encouragingly to Kim before leaving the two strangers alone.

Kim awkwardly stood beside the door. During all her research, Dorothy was nothing more than a name. A subject to study. Now Kim was reminded that Dorothy was a *real* person. A person with feelings and emotions.

Maybe this wasn't such a good idea...

"Well, are you going to visit me or just test the air quality?" Dorothy snapped.

Kim was taken aback by the abrupt words and hastily replied, "Um, hello. My name is Kim..."

"Yes, I was just told your name and unless my memory is getting as poor as you suggest, your last name is Lawson."

"Um, do you mind if I sit down, please?"

"Do you always begin your sentences with the word, um?"

"I hadn't noticed I was."

"Live and learn I always say. And yes, you may."

"I may what?" asked Kim.

Dorothy slowly turned around in her seat and eyed Kim through her large framed glasses.

"Sit down." She pronounced each word slowly and clearly.

"Oh. Thank you." She quickly took a seat on the edge of the nicely made bed. Kim decided the best thing to do was to be blunt.

As she pulled out the letters from her purse, she said, "I have something for you."

Dorothy raised her eye brows in surprise when she saw the stack. "I haven't received a letter in ages. How is that possible?"

"I live at thirty-seven Millington Lane in Cedarville. I found these in the attic when my husband and I were cleaning it out."

The old woman's eyes had a spark of light in them now and she stared at Kim with new interest.

"The big green house? Is there still a tire swing in the backyard?"

Kim smiled. "Yes ma'am."

Dorothy shook her head quickly. "Don't call me ma'am. Just Dorothy will do. May I?"

Kim nodded and held them out. Dorothy looked at them cautiously at first; as if afraid they would reach out and strike her. Gathering her courage, Dorothy took the letters with shaking hands. She fingered the delicate rose.

Kim settled down comfortably and watched as the old woman worked at untying the twine.

The next few minutes were silent as Dorothy opened and poured over each letter. Kim could not help but notice there were tears in the woman's eyes.

Finally, Dorothy looked up from her mail. Her eyes were closed and a smile of both joy and sorrow was plain to see. Kim said nothing. After a minute, Dorothy seemed to return from whatever memory or time she had visited and remembered the messenger who sat across from her.

"My dear girl. Do you want to hear a story?"

Kim nodded eagerly. This was what she'd been waiting for from the very beginning.

"I won't bore you with all the details, but I grew up in that house, the one you own now. I was but a young girl then. Oh, was it so long ago?" She paused as she touched her wrinkled hands to her face.

Dorothy continued. "My family was very well off. My mother always told me that before I was born, she practically had to claw her way into society. I was convinced that she was determined that nothing, not even my happiness would drag her back down. I was dragged to all the social events and parties. I was expected to marry a man of my mother's choosing but I feel in love with a drug store clerk. Thomas." Dorothy chuckled. "I haven't said that name aloud in years."

"When my mother found out about us, she was livid and forbid us to marry."

Dorothy sighed. "Thomas was drafted in World War two and my heart nearly broke. We promised each other that someday we'd be together. He left to serve his country and I refused to attend a single social event as a form of rebellion."

"The years passed and the war continued. I held onto the hope of our promise until I received a telegram saying that my Tom was killed in action. Little did I know that this was a lie. Somehow my mother had paid off an official to make up this telegram so I would give up my stubborn ways. I didn't find this out until after the war ended, after I was already married to the stuffy and boorish Mr. McCarthy. Tom was celebrated in the newspaper as a war hero."

Kim had to interrupt. "Wait. Didn't he try to see you or find you when he got back home?"

Dorothy shook her head. "I believe my mother got to him and told him I was already married."

"Did you try to get a divorce?"

"My dear girl, people didn't divorce back in that day. Especially in high society. It would have tarnished the reputation."

Kim pointed to the letters. "So, what are those then?"

Dorothy smiled like a small child. "Love letters he sent me before he left for the war. There's a lovely story behind the rose but that's for another time. I kept all of these together in my hope chest but oddly enough, just before I was to be married, these disappeared. I knew my mother had stolen them, but I could never prove it.

"Thank you, for bringing my Tom back to me," Dorothy said softly. "I'll treasure this forever."

"Do you think we can find him?" Kim wondered aloud.

Dorothy smiled sadly. "No, my dear, I'm afraid he's long gone. Died of a heart attack back in the sixties. He never did marry."

"I'm so sorry, Dorothy."

"Don't be sorry. Believe me; I've spent too many years feeling sorry for myself. You have given me more than anyone could and I thank you with all my heart for it."

Kim smiled. "I'm glad I could do it. I guess I'd better be going."

Dorothy inquired about the old house and Kim gently explained its poor condition. "That's why we were cleaning out the attic. The house is going to be demolished in a few weeks."

"Such a shame. But nothing lasts forever." Dorothy hugged her letters. "I'm thankful to have these at least. Please come see me if you come back to the area."

Kim promised she would and left shortly after. That evening, Dorothy Kingsley lay in her bed, hugging her letters and the rose close to her heart. She passed away peacefully in her sleep with a smile on her face.

End

Keep Swinging

The girl takes a seat on the swing. Her fingers tighten around the chains. She slowly inches backwards to prepare for takeoff. Her shoes dig into the gravel, the crunch of the pea-size gravel is pleasant to the ear.

Once she is as far back as she can go, she lifts her feet and sails forward. Her short brown hair moves slightly in the breeze but she is not satisfied.

Pumping her legs, she goes back and forth, higher and faster each time. She has the rhythm now and never misses a beat. If others are around her, she takes no notice.

She closes her eyes and tilts her head back. At first the sensation is frightening but she does not stop. Higher and further she swings.

When she opens her eyes, the clouds seem so close; close enough to touch. Once the swing goes forward, she determines within herself to reach out to the wispy white cloud.

Closer she comes now; she holds tight with one hand on the metal chain and reaches out another to the cloud. To her pleasant surprise, her hand feels moist and damp. The girl smiles with satisfaction at achieving the unexpected.

She again closes her eyes and keeps swinging. Her legs continue to pump and the breeze on her skin is heavenly.

Now she opens her eyes and lets out a gasp. She holds tightly to both chains and beams at how far she has come. Below her are oceans, mountains, deserts and her home. Yes, from here she looks down on Earth.

Up above and all around, she clearly sees the stars, bright and glorious. Leaning her head back and twisting in her seat to look behind, she sees not only stars, but swirls of galaxies and colors she didn't even know existed. She keeps pumping her legs, never wanting to leave. The galaxies are quiet and serene.

A thrilling thought occurs to her. If I close my eyes again, I may end up on another planet!

She takes one last fond look down at Earth before closing her eyes for the last time. She continues to pump her legs, feeling she is going higher and higher.

Suddenly her feet make contact with something. Excitement swells up within her and she opens her eyes.

Her built up joy is sadly dashed as she looks around in bewilderment. Beneath her gym shoes are gravel rocks. All around her other children are running and playing. She looks up and sees the same puffy white clouds. Gravity has a firm hold of her again and she feels the weight of it.

From the school building, a harsh bell rings; ordering the children to leave the free air and return to the stuffy classrooms. She dreads leaving the playground.

She slowly stands and takes a few steps from her swing. Gazing up at the heavens, she sighs, and then looks back to her swing.

A smile of anticipation creeps over her and she confidentially says, "Tomorrow, I'll go even further."

With that she takes off running to the school building, her arms out and her imagination still flying high.

End

The End

"Penny? Love, wake up."

The gentle sound of her mom's voice penetrated through her dreams of heroes and villains and she slowly awoke. Her body was stiff and cramped from being curled up in the chair for so long.

Easing herself up in the chair, Penny froze and looked down. She wasn't in the big red arm chair. She was sitting on a dusty-coated drape. Lifting the fabric, she saw a broken down brown chair. Stuffing and springs were poking through the aged material.

Penny's mother noticed the alarm in her daughter's face. "Are you alright? What were you doing sleeping in this creepy room, when you had the guest room to stay in?"

"But it wasn't creepy last night..." Her voice trailed off as she scanned the room. Cobwebs lined the walls; they were so thick that they blocked off entire sections of the room. The tile floor was cracked and crumbling away. The fireplace that had seemed so cheerful just hours ago was now boarded up. In place of great uncle Morris' portrait, was a shelf that held a vase with a few rotten flowers, a human skull, and a stuffed raven.

Penny whirled around and was relieved to see that the bookcase was still there. But it was now overflowing with books, their spines cloaked in dust, held together by cobwebs, and sprinkled with mildew.

"It was dark," mom offered. "You know how things look differently in the dark."

Penny refused to admit this was the case. It was impossible that this was the same room she'd fell asleep in while reading.

The book! Penny stood up and began searching under the drape and on the floor beneath the chair.

"Penny? What are you looking for?"

"A book I was reading. I got it from that bookcase."

Her mom cast a skeptical look at the bookcase. "Love? Are you okay?"

The book was nowhere to be found. Penny scratched her head. Could it have all been a dream? The fire and the portrait? And the book?

Mom put an arm around Penny's shoulder. "Dad's packing the car. It's time for us to go home."

"How's Aunt Winnie?"

Mom sighed and shook her head. "She passed on early this morning. We called for an ambulance and they took her away."

"I'm sorry."

"It's alright, love. How about we go grab a hot breakfast at a cafe?"

Penny nodded. Breakfast sounded good. She followed her mom across the room, but stopped when she came to the door. Penny took one last look at the mysterious room before leaving.

The family drove away in their car and the house was once again left to its own devices.

Had Penny checked the bookcase thoroughly, she would have known that by pushing on it ever so slightly, it would open, revealing the cozy little room in which a goblin called Crumpet, named by great uncle Morris because of the creature's obsession with the treat, lived.

Last night, Crumpet accidently forgot to close the entrance to his room, allowing Penny to blindly walk in.

Alone and happy once more, Crumpet reclaimed his chair and settled in to read from his favorite book.

Penny's forgotten flashlight was on the floor beside him, handy for reading in the dark.

The End

Did you enjoy reading The Bookcase Collection?

Please take a moment to leave a review on Amazon or Goodreads and share this with your friends

If you enjoyed this, consider checking out my other stand-alone books:

The Beast:

Not for the faint of heart! A gripping thriller about a family stalked by a killer panther. Captive in their home, they face starvation, nightmares, and more.

Puzzlers:

Three short mysteries that will keep you guessing until the end.

Welcome to Ludicrous:

Need a laugh? Welcome to a town where everything is backwards. The butcher is a vegetarian and the exterminator is terrified of bugs.

24 Hour Lockdown:

Six strangers are locked down in a public library for a grueling 24 hours. Expect laughs, arguments and maybe murder...

The Roman Road:

Romans 3:23

Roman 5:8

Roman 6:23

Romans 10:9-10

Ephesians 2:8-9

Made in the USA
Monee, IL
15 June 2020